W9-BCI-713

THE
POPULARITY
CODE

THE POPULARITY CODE

STEPHANIE FARIS

ALADDIN

New York London Toronto Sydney New Delhi

This book is a work of fiction. Any references to historical events, real people, or real places are used fictitiously. Other names, characters, places, and events are products of the author's imagination, and any resemblance to actual events or places or persons, living or dead, is entirely coincidental.

ALADDIN
An imprint of Simon & Schuster Children's Publishing Division
1230 Avenue of the Americas, New York, New York 10020
First Aladdin hardcover edition April 2020
Text copyright © 2020 by Stephanie Faris
Jacket illustration copyright © 2020 by Erika Pajarillo
Also available in an Aladdin paperback edition.
All rights reserved, including the right of reproduction in whole or in part in any form.
ALADDIN and related logo are registered trademarks of Simon & Schuster, Inc.
For information about special discounts for bulk purchases, please contact Simon & Schuster
Special Sales at 1-866-506-1949 or business@simonandschuster.com.
The Simon & Schuster Speakers Bureau can bring authors to your live event. For more information
or to book an event contact the Simon & Schuster Speakers Bureau at 1-866-248-3049 or visit our
website at www.simonspeakers.com.
Designed by Heather Palisi
The text of this book was set in Chronicle Display.
Manufactured in the United States of America 0320 FFG
2 4 6 8 10 9 7 5 3 1
Library of Congress Cataloging-in-Publication Data
Names: Faris, Stephanie, author.
Title: The popularity code / Stephanie Faris.
Description: First Aladdin paperback edition. | New York : Aladdin, 2020. |
Audience: Ages 9-13. | Audience: Grades 4-6. | Summary: When the students in her middle school
become obsessed with a new website called SlamBook, Faith Taylor decides to find out which
classmates are leaving negative posts and retaliates with her own harmful comments.
Identifiers: LCCN 2020000537 (print) | LCCN 2020000538 (eBook) |
ISBN 9781534445208 (hc) | ISBN 9781534445192 (pbk) | ISBN 9781534445215 (eBook)
Subjects: CYAC: Social media—Fiction. | Cyberbullying—Fiction. |
Computer programming—Fiction. | Popularity—Fiction. | Revenge—Fiction. |
Depression, Mental—Fiction. | Middle schools. | Schools.
Classification: LCC PZ7.F22705 Po 2020 (print) | LCC PZ7.F22705 (eBook) | DDC [Fic]—dc23
LC record available at https://lccn.loc.gov/2020000537
LC eBook record available at https://lccn.loc.gov/2020000538

For Marquita. So thankful to have you as both a mother-in-law and a friend

CHAPTER 1

Breakfast at the Taylor house was never boring. There was my father, standing in front of the open refrigerator in his robe, reading an email on his smartphone. There was my sister, sitting next to me at the table and posing while she tested her new selfie ring light on her phone. And then there was me, eating my cereal while trying to figure out why all the hard work I'd done the night before had been for absolutely nothing.

Yes, we had a "no screens at the table" rule in my family. And yes, when my mom came blowing in like a hurricane in a few minutes, we'd all be in trouble. But between homework and school, I hadn't had enough time to figure out why the app I'd spent hours coding was completely broken.

Sure enough, my mom came breezing in when I was halfway through my bowl of Wheat-e-os. A great day starts with a healthy breakfast and all that. My goal was just to wolf it down so I could get back to my work, but if Mom saw me rushing, I wouldn't be able to do that. Eating fast while trying to look like you weren't was really, really hard.

"Phone down, Hope," Mom said, tapping the button to warm up the coffee maker as she whipped past it on her way to the fridge. "And, Faith, a laptop? Really?"

My parents, in a complete fit of unoriginality, had named my older sister Hope, then named me Faith a couple of years later. Someone really should have stopped them.

"I worked for hours on this," I said without taking my eyes off my screen. "I can't figure out why it's broken."

My sister sighed. She didn't get me. It was like we were from two completely different sets of parents. If I hadn't looked so much like my dad and Hope hadn't looked like a younger version of my mom, I'd have had to check to see if one of us was adopted.

😊 2

"I don't care if you have the winning lottery numbers. No screens at the table," Mom said. She had already shooed Dad out of the way and was on her way back to the coffee maker with the soy milk. "It's rude."

I closed my laptop and slid it off to the side. If I speed-ate my Wheat-e-os, I could take my bowl to the sink and get back onto my laptop somewhere other than the table. Just a few more minutes of focus were all I needed.

"Is this the homework app?" Mom asked as the coffee maker noisily spat out her organic decaffeinated beverage. "The one your mentor wants to send to her friend?"

My coding club coach supposedly had a friend who worked for Google. And *that* friend was just going to love an app that let students help each other do homework. Google would buy it and pay me millions, and we'd get our Paris trip. Either that or my coding coach's friend was, like, a guy who cleaned toilets at Google and wouldn't care anything about my app. I wouldn't know for sure until I finished the app and shared it.

"Yeah, that's going to take a while," I said. Staring longingly at the laptop I'd been forced to set aside, I shoved down as much cereal as I could fit into my mouth. Just a few more bites and I could get away from the table. It was all about getting back to my code at this point.

"What did I tell you about positive thinking?" Mom asked, walking to the table. She set her coffee cup down and pulled her chair out. "If you think it will take a while, it will. If you think you'll be finished tomorrow, you'll be finished tomorrow."

I laughed at the same time that I swallowed, briefly feeling like I was going to choke. If I choked, Mom would make me slow down and eat like a civilized human being.

"I can assure you, it will not be finished tomorrow," I finally said when I could once again take a breath. *"But . . . if I could eat and work at the same time, maybe . . ."*

"Nice try," Mom said. "Craig, tell Faith about positive thoughts."

Dad took his spot at the table. He was fully dressed in dark jeans and a golf shirt, his phone safely holstered in the case on his belt.

"Positive thoughts put positive energy into the universe," Dad said. "Or something like that."

I smiled. Dad and I were a lot alike. We were both practical and into science and math and all that brainy stuff. Hope was more like my mom, even though she didn't eat as healthfully as Mom and I did. But she was a dedicated cheerleader who spent all her spare time taking gymnastics, so she had the physical fitness part of it *down*. She even took my mom's yoga class on weekends sometimes.

Suddenly I looked down and found that my cereal bowl was all milk. I wanted to make sure I finished every bite so Mom would have no excuse to say that I couldn't hop back onto my laptop.

I got up and walked to the sink, then dumped the remaining soy milk down the drain and put my dish and spoon into the dishwasher. No excuses.

"Who's riding with me?" Dad asked, grabbing a cold coffee out of the refrigerator and unscrewing the cap.

Wait . . . what? It was time to go already? I weighed my options. I could stay home and try to get some time in on my laptop in the ten minutes it took for the bus to arrive. Or I could ride with Dad and smuggle my laptop into school and hide out in one of the empty classrooms, hoping my friends didn't find me in there. Once they found me, I'd get no work done.

"Me!" I called out.

"I'll take the bus," Hope said. She was finishing up her banana while staring longingly at her phone.

"See you after school!" Mom called out to me. She always picked me up from school after her afternoon class, since I didn't have after-school activities like Hope did. Sometimes we even stopped for frozen custard and fruit. Mom loved custard.

Dad always left his car parked in the driveway, letting Mom have the garage. He said it kept her from having to be out in the cold and heat and rain. I always made gagging noises when Mom and Dad were all romantic like that, but secretly I liked it that they were so sweet to each other.

"Your mom may be onto something," Dad commented as he backed out of the driveway. "This app could be the big one."

"I'm trying not to get my hopes up," I said absently.

Dad always got his hopes up. As practical and analytical as he was, he was a dreamer. Which was an interesting contrast. He was sure he was going to come up with some invention that would make us all rich. That was why he spent most of his free time working in the tiny office that was also our guest bedroom. He was always gluing things together or building things out of parts.

"Can I ask you a question?" I asked Dad.

"You just did."

That threw me for a second. Then I got it. My father had what you might call a dorky sense of humor. It was the kind of humor that made you groan because if anyone you knew overheard it, you'd be mortified. If nobody else heard it, it was admittedly kind of cute.

"When did you know what you wanted to be when you grew up?" I asked.

Full disclosure: I had no idea what my dad did for a living. I mean, I knew he was a mechanical engineer, but I had no idea what that meant. Did he work on engines or something? Whatever he did, it was something that had him going to an office every day and sitting alone at a desk for hours. That was why he could wear jeans to work. I figured, when he wasn't at his computer, he was writing on big whiteboards while other people sat around and oohed and aahed over how brilliant his ideas were.

Dad laughed. "I'm still not sure I know. When I was your age, I wanted to be a rock star."

What? That was the freakiest thing I'd ever heard. Aside from his cheesy jokes, my father was all serious all the time.

"Like Ed Sheeran?" I asked. I could see a younger version of Dad with a beard and guitar. Add some tattoos, and he *might* look like a singer.

"More like Nickelback," he said. "Ed Sheeran wasn't a thing when I was a kid."

I didn't know who Nickelback was. I figured I probably didn't want to know.

"So when did you know you wanted to be a mechanical engineer?"

"I always liked to build things," he said with a shrug.

He launched into a long story about when he was five and he built a fake high-rise with a bunch of Legos. It only reinforced my idea that I'd gotten my coding skills from Dad. We both enjoyed building things.

He finished up his story with, "And when I got to college, I just took a bunch of engineering classes until I figured out what I wanted to do with my degree."

I thought about that for a second. I'd known for a long time that I wanted to be a computer programmer. But sometimes I wondered if it might be nice to try something else. Maybe I could train to be an astronaut or study medicine and become a doctor. I didn't have to decide right now, did I?

"Isn't that your friend?" Dad asked, calling my attention to the fact that we were now pulling up to the front of the school. People were all around, walking toward the entrance, but I honed right in on Tierra Ford. The girl my dad had just called my "friend."

The thing was, Tierra *had been* my friend. Only, Dad was off by a few months. When my family had first moved, Tierra had been the first friend I'd made. We sat next to each other in third grade, and soon we were doing everything together. We probably would have stayed BFFs until graduation if I hadn't met Janelle in my mom's yoga class over the summer. Janelle walked in, saw I was the only person her age, and plopped her mat down next to me. We eventually started hanging out after class, and soon she introduced me to her best friend, Adria.

I spent the summer hanging out with them, mostly, and started hanging out with Tierra less and less. By the time school started, Tierra and I hadn't spoken in months. I did my best to ignore the hurt in her eyes, but she didn't confront me on it. It was like we had an agreement that we weren't friends anymore.

"Yeah," I said. "See you after school."

I opened the door and stepped out.

"Wait!" Dad called out.

I was all prepared to bolt for the school entrance, pretending I didn't see Tierra sitting there, so I was already in "rush" mode. But I stopped myself just as I was about to slam the car door shut. I leaned in.

"Aren't you forgetting something?" he asked.

What? I didn't get it. Was this some trick to get me to say I loved him or something?

"Your backpack," he said, shifting his eyes toward the floorboard of the passenger seat. Sure enough, I'd completely forgotten my backpack.

"Thanks!" I said, grabbing it. Then I gave him a wave before swinging the door shut.

Now, to get past Tierra.

I slung my backpack over one shoulder and took off like a rocket. I could walk pretty fast when I set my mind to it. It didn't hurt that it was super chilly outside, and nobody wanted to be out there longer than necessary. That thought brought an important question, though. Why was Tierra sitting on the bench outside the school, wearing nothing but a fleece jacket?

I kept my attention focused forward as I got closer, but out of the corner of my eye, I could see her. She pulled her feet up onto the bench, which put her knees close to her face. Then she seemed to hide behind her arms, which she folded over the tops of her knees.

She was hiding from me?

I saw her hand wipe over her cheek. She was crying.

My stomach flip-flopped. As great as it was to hang out with my new friends, it was just, like, a *minute* before that Tierra had been my best friend. That didn't just go away because I was suddenly (kind of) part of the popular crowd.

Before I could even think about it, I started walking toward her. As I got closer, she put her feet back onto the ground and sat up straight, wiping both her cheeks with the back of her hand.

"Are you okay?" I asked.

She looked up at me then, and I realized why I'd stopped to talk to her. There was a time in third grade when Tierra had been invited to a birthday party and I hadn't been. Instead of going without me, she'd turned down the invite and taken me to get our nails done. That was what a real friend did.

And after that, I'd been a horrible, horrible friend.

"I'm fine," she said. "Just go inside."

I should have taken her up on her offer. I should have gotten out of there while I had the chance. But I kept thinking about all the other things she'd done for me too. The times she'd stood up for me when boys had been picking on me, or how she'd helped me fit in with other girls in our class.

I sat down on the bench next to her. I might have found new friends, but I wasn't heartless. Tierra was a good person. We'd just drifted apart. That stuff happened in middle school. It happened after middle school too, I was pretty sure.

"Sometimes it feels good to cry," I said. "It's like you're getting the pain out. Through your tears."

That was easily the sappiest, most clichéd thing I'd ever said. But I had no idea what else to say. I should have been inside the school, finding an empty classroom where

I could hide for the next half hour or so. Instead I was sitting there with someone who didn't even want to talk about why she was crying.

"People just suck," Tierra said. "That's all."

She wiped at her cheek again, and I realized the tears hadn't stopped. That made me feel awkward all over again.

"They do," I said. "Did someone say something mean to you? Do you want me to beat them up?"

"Why do you care?" she asked.

She had every right to be mad at me. I'd be mad at me too, if I were her. I sighed and said the only thing I could think to say.

"Whatever it is, I'm sure it'll pass," I said. "You could just take the day off. Maybe play sick?"

She said nothing. Just sat there, staring straight ahead. I felt a pang I had no right to feel. A longing for the friendship we'd had just a few months earlier.

I looked around for a clue to what was going on. It was so early. How could something have already happened that upset her? I didn't get it.

Then I noticed the phone next to her on the bench. Maybe someone had texted her something. Or someone had tagged her on Twitter or Instagram. Those were the only things I could imagine that would make her cry.

"I'm a good listener," I reminded her.

To be honest, I kind of missed having a really good friend who got me. And I knew Tierra had every right to be furious at me. I wouldn't have been surprised if she'd told me to leave her alone. I probably deserved that. But instead she sighed and picked up her phone, unlocking it with her thumb.

"Faith!"

I looked past Tierra to see Adria standing near the entrance, holding the door to the school open.

I felt like I'd been caught doing something wrong. Like stealing. Or lying. Or sneaking my sister's favorite ice cream from the freezer when I thought she was asleep. It was silly, but Janelle and Adria knew I'd once been friends with Tierra, and it didn't stop them from making fun of her. All. The. Time.

"I have to go," I said.

I felt like a completely horrible person as soon as the words were out of my mouth, but what else could I do? I needed my two BFFs. Janelle was the girl everyone wanted to be like. Everything she wore, said, and did was just perfect. Adria could be mean sometimes, but she was Janelle's best friend, so they came as a package. If I wasn't friends with Janelle, I'd go back to being a total nobody.

"Yeah, whatever," Tierra said, staring intently at her screen.

I knew that the right thing to do would be to stay with Tierra and tell Adria I'd be right in. But I didn't do that. Why? Because Adria was staring me down, and I got nervous. I hopped up and rushed toward the front door, tossing my backpack over my shoulder as I walked. Not a second to waste.

I didn't dare look back at Tierra, and I tried not to think about what had made her cry. It was easier to just focus on hanging out with my friends and being happy.

CHAPTER 2

"I've sent you, like, seventy texts. What's the deal?"

Adria started in a total of five seconds after we were inside the school. We were walking past the trophy case, and she was holding up her phone. Sure enough, there was a screen full of texts that basically read, **Hello?** and **Where R U?**

"We have a nine-one-one sitch," Adria said, gesturing for us to take a hard left to head toward the area where Adria and Janelle shared a locker. Adria actually had her own locker, but she'd moved her stuff on the first day of school. I was pretty sure Janelle was too afraid to say no.

"What's up?" I asked, unlocking my phone. I didn't really want to go through all the texts, so if she could just summarize the "sitch," that would be *great*.

"There's this awful website," Adria said. "It's just—you have to see it."

"Send me the link," I said, scrolling through my text messages. Maybe the link was there.

"Janelle's in the media center," she said. "Come on."

Adria took off, leaving me to try to catch up. She was weaving through groups of kids, shouting "Hey" back to all the people calling out to us, and basically looking like a person on a mission. Her mission was to show me some website?

I realized, as we rushed, just how easy it was for me to forget about Tierra and the old me. Before summer, nobody would have even glanced at me as I walked down the hall. I'd been totally invisible. Now people knew my name. People I didn't even know. It was nice to feel like I mattered.

I glanced at the time on my phone. We had about ten minutes before the first bell would ring. So much for getting to school early. And now instead of talking about important stuff like what we we'd watched on the TV last night, we were going to be looking at some *website*?

The media center was almost empty this time of morning. A couple of students were doing last-minute homework, and one was playing online, but otherwise the place was deserted. Janelle was seated at a computer near the window.

"Hey," I said as we got closer. Even though I'd spoken in a near whisper, it had sounded like a scream in that chamber of silence.

"Ohmigosh, it's gotten worse," Janelle said. "Get over here."

Adria pulled a chair as close to Janelle's as she could get and plopped down into it. I settled for just hunkering down next to Janelle's shoulder. We didn't have that long to stand there, and maybe if I didn't commit to a chair, this would last just a few seconds. Then we could get back to having fun.

The smile that was on my face vanished when I saw the name at the top of the page. Janelle Tenning.

What? Wait. Why was Janelle's name at the top of a website?

Below her name was a list of things I didn't understand. *Sweet, hottie, love her, adorbs, so cute . . .*

"I don't understand," I said. "What is this?"

"It's called a slam book," Adria said. "This was what I was texting you about."

Our school blocked some websites on the media center computers, but apparently not this one. Maybe it was so new, it had gotten around the filters somehow?

"Someone did a whole webpage about you?" I asked Janelle.

"I don't know," Janelle said. "It looks like anyone can comment, though."

"Well, you have to log in first," Adria said. "Whoever created this site will see your sign-up name. You're supposed to give your real name too, but only the administrator can see it."

"If you don't give your real name, they can delete your comments," Janelle explained, looking up at Adria. "I didn't mention that when I talked to you."

"There are pages for other people too," Adria told me, probably noticing that I still looked confused. "Not us yet."

I wasn't sure whether to be glad or upset about that.

I didn't really want a page with my name at the top, but why wasn't there a page about Adria? Why Janelle and not her? I was kind of new to not being invisible, but Adria had been hanging out with Janelle forever. Just how long did someone have to be Janelle's friend before being just as important?

I was pretty sure if I asked anyone in school that question, they'd say it would never happen. Janelle was more interesting than everyone else. It was obvious from this webpage she'd just shown us that everyone thought she was the sweetest, prettiest, most perfect person ever. Unless the point of the page was just to say nice things about people. If so, that was kind of awesome.

"Ugh," Janelle said, clicking the big *X* to close the window and log off the computer. "I don't want to see any more."

Janelle was upset over being called "pretty" and "adorbs"? I didn't get it. I'd take it if she didn't want it, though.

"I have an idea," Adria said while Janelle was getting her stuff together to leave the media center. "We should all create accounts and post only nice things about you."

"And everyone else," I said.

 20

Silence. Janelle even paused, midway through standing up, to stare at me.

Okay. Apparently they weren't on board with posting nice comments about everyone else.

"I'm being serious," Adria said, as if what I'd said had been some huge joke. "We can post great things like, 'Janelle *lives* to help others' and 'Nobody is as nice as Janelle.'"

"Umm . . . the comments aren't really full sentences," I pointed out. "They're phrases, like 'so cute,' or words, like 'sweet.'"

"Right," Janelle said. "We need to come up with one-word descriptions of me, like 'supersweet.'"

"Those are two words, I think?" Adria said.

"A compound word," I blurted out, then wondered if that had made me sound like a know-it-all. But they didn't say anything.

We exited the media center, probably making everyone in there happy for the silence again, and headed out into the crowded hallway. Janelle started waving, and soon she was surrounded by people, flashing her bright smile at everyone she passed. She was on the cheerleading squad, which was equal to being royalty at school. Everyone knew who she was and seemed to think she was supposed to know who they were too.

"I wonder who wrote those things about her," Adria said under her breath as we walked.

I knew exactly what she meant. Suddenly the people all around us weren't classmates and friends. They could very well be the same people who had posted about Janelle.

We couldn't even make it to our lockers without Janelle stopping to talk to someone. So we went on without her.

"Do you think they'll do pages about us?" I asked. "Maybe if we log in, someone will realize we don't have pages yet."

I did *not* want a page where people wrote about me. I knew there was no way the comments would be gushy like Janelle's were. Besides, even if they said mean things about her, she'd handle it better than I would. She knew she was awesome, no matter what people said about her. If mean things were written about me, I probably would believe them.

"There aren't many pages right now," Adria said. "I

 22

hope ours are coming soon. If not, we're total losers."

That was the point where we parted to go to our separate lockers, which gave me a minute or two to think about that. We'd be losers if we didn't get a page soon? So now our reputation depended on some silly website where people posted gossipy things about other people? Something seemed wrong with that.

I grabbed my items from my locker quickly and rushed to Janelle and Adria's locker. They were standing together when I arrived. They were deep in conversation.

"Meet at my house after school," Janelle told me as I approached. "We'll create accounts and figure out what we're going to do."

"Why don't we just do that at lunch on our phones?" I asked. Not that I didn't want to hang out after school. It just seemed like a long time away.

"No!" Janelle called out just as I was unlocking my phone.

Adria reached out to put her hand on my phone. "Janelle doesn't want anyone to see us looking at the site."

Oh. Good point. There were people all around, and even if we hid the phone screen, someone could catch us looking at the website. People talked. That was probably why Janelle had gone to the library that morning and hidden in the back corner rather than having us look at the phone in the hallway. We could do it in hiding somewhere during lunch, but I didn't have time to argue with them. People were starting to scatter, so I knew the warning bell was only seconds away.

"It's a plan," I said, stepping away from my friends. I had to get to class early to find the paper I had due today and read over it one last time before the final bell.

"Let's go," Janelle said. She was in homeroom with me and all the other people whose last name started with *T*.

Alone with Janelle, I felt like I could finally breathe again. Adria was great, but she could sometimes be . . . *overbearing* when Janelle was around. I usually liked it better when I was alone with one of them. With all three of us, it felt too much like I had to compete with Adria for Janelle's attention.

"It just feels icky," Janelle said, speaking quietly so that only I could hear. "Like, a violation, right? People are writing about me where everyone can see."

"Don't worry about it," I said. "It just means you're awesome enough that people want to say great things about you."

"I think someone did it just to get to me," she said, looking over her shoulder to make sure nobody was listening.

I doubted someone had set up a website just to get to Janelle. As popular as she was, we were, after all, just seventh graders. If that slam book thing had more people on it, I was betting there were sixth and eighth graders too. Not just people from our class.

"What if someone writes something mean?" Janelle asked. "Do you think they'll take it down?"

I nodded. "Definitely."

I had no idea, but I said it with full confidence. I had to admit, I felt a little boost that Janelle was asking my advice. Over the summer our friendship had become pretty strong, but back in school things had changed immediately. Like at any second someone would tell me it was a mistake. I was supposed to be sitting at that lunch table with Tierra, not with everyone who was *someone* in seventh grade.

But I knew exactly how Janelle felt as we walked into homeroom. It was hard to look at people without wondering who else had seen the slam book site. And if there was ever a page about me, would even one thing be half as nice as what people had written about Janelle?

"Hay-yay!"

Amy Tatem. She was always there, always overly happy to see us. Janelle specifically. And she seemed to have a way of dragging the word "hey" into two syllables.

"Hi!" Janelle said.

Was it my imagination, or was Janelle being even nicer than usual? Was she making an extra effort to be nice to everyone? Did she think that she could influence people to write nice things about her on the slam book site?

I probably could be influenced to write nice things about her.

"So did you hear about JoJo Maxwell?" Amy asked, leaning forward so only the two of us would hear.

Gossip. Great. Just what this morning needed.

"No," Janelle said, opening her notebook.

That reminded me that I needed to look over my paper. I turned to face forward again, opening my folder to pull the paper out. My grade was still at a B, and I really wanted an A in history this semester. This paper could do it.

"She was caught cheating. Five days' suspension."

"That's awful," Janelle said.

"She copied Tierra Ford's English paper. Tierra said she didn't know, but everyone kind of thinks she was in on it."

I looked over at Amy, my paper forgotten. "Did you say 'Tierra Ford'?" I asked.

"Yes," she said. "Why?"

Suddenly she looked interested in me. Not Janelle but me. I knew it was only because she thought I had some juicy piece of gossip. I thought about it for a second. If I told her Tierra had been crying that morning, Amy would latch on to what I was saying like I was the most interesting person ever.

No, I couldn't. That would make me as gossipy as Amy.

"Nothing," I said. "We just used to be friends."

"I remember," Amy said. "You guys were joined at the hip. And then you met Janelle."

"And I saved her!" Janelle said with a big smile.

My eyes widened. *Saved* me. Huh.

Homeroom started then, forcing an end to the conversation. As I waited through the morning announcements, though, I thought about what Janelle had said. In a way, she *had* saved me. Now that I was hanging out with

Janelle, people were starting to pay attention to me. They just treated me like the friend of someone awesome, pretty much, but that was better than being totally ignored.

But being friends with Tierra *had* been great. She was fun to be around, and we had a ton in common. More in common than I had with Janelle, and especially more than I had with Adria.

Take hanging out at the pool, for instance. With Tierra, we actually went swimming. We didn't just sit around in sunglasses, looking around to see if any boys were watching us, but we had fun. We did gymnastics at the indoor trampoline park and went to the fair and ate cotton candy without worrying about it making our jeans fit too tightly. With Tierra, I could always be myself.

With Janelle and Adria, I felt like I was always trying to prove I was good enough.

I thought about Tierra so much in homeroom that when I saw her on the way to first period, I felt bad. Like she knew I'd been thinking about how we weren't friends anymore. I was almost glad to get to first period, where I could read over my paper and not talk to anyone for a few minutes.

Only, I didn't read my paper. Instead I pulled out my phone and typed in the web address I'd seen at the top of Janelle's page. I scrolled through the page on Janelle, saw that nothing had changed, and then clicked the title to go to the main page.

Welcome to SlamBook! it said in big, bold letters at the top. Like I'd just stumbled upon something warm and friendly, not a page meant to "slam" middle-school girls. And why was "SlamBook" written as one word? Was it a play on "Facebook," maybe?

I quickly scrolled down to read the rest. Class was going to start soon, so I had to hurry.

Have you ever wondered what other people think of you—what people are saying behind your back? Well, this is your chance to find out. Some of the most talked-about Gladesville Middle School students are listed here. If you don't see your name, you probably suck.

Below that were instructions on how to create an account and comment. All accounts were verified by the administrator before approval. You didn't have to give your name, but you had to answer a bunch of questions. I winced. I didn't really want to do that, but it seemed like

Adria would probably make me. The second we left nice comments about Janelle, the person in charge of all of this would know it was us. She might even take the comments down, which would mean we'd created an account . . . and called attention to ourselves . . . for nothing.

At least I wouldn't suck if the administrator created a page for us. There was that.

Below the note telling us we sucked was a list of names. Most of them I didn't recognize, probably because they weren't seventh graders. Janelle, all the other cheerleaders, some girls from the dance team, and a few football and basketball players were all that I saw from seventh grade.

I started clicking through names, but I couldn't figure out how slams would work. Like, once I created an account, would I just find people and start writing things about them? Did they have to be nice things? It said you could see what people were saying behind your back, so they couldn't guarantee it would all be good, right?

It was so confusing.

And if I thought it couldn't get any more confusing, I was wrong. I figured that out in the cafeteria at lunch, as

I stood in line behind two girls talking about SlamBook. They weren't even keeping their voices down. It was like they didn't care who overheard them talking about it.

"It's so mean," one of the girls said.

"But so fun," said the other. "Did you see what they wrote about Damen King? I hope he sees it. He's kind of full of himself."

"Kind of? You think?"

I glanced back over my shoulder at Janelle and Adria, who were sitting at the table, picking over their grapes and celery. I wasn't much for their low-calorie lunches. Besides, today was pizza quesadilla day. That was my favorite.

"I heard that they're adding a bunch more people," said the girl who thought Damen King was kind of full of himself. "All the popular people."

I frowned. I never thought of myself as popular, but all I had to do was turn around to look at Janelle and Adria to see where I stood. They were in the center of a long table that would soon be teeming with all the seventh graders who were considered popular.

"I have a few people I could suggest," I heard the other girl say. "There's a lot of *mean* going on around here."

It was time for the two girls to order, so they had to stop talking. I didn't know for sure if they saw me back there, but I wanted to disappear.

Somehow I made it through the line and back to the table where my friends were sitting. They were hunched together, talking about something. When they saw me, they went silent.

That happened a lot. It always reminded me that we may have hung out together, but Adria was Janelle's friend, not mine. Even though I didn't have as much in common with Janelle as Adria did, I still felt a bond with her. Now I only felt that bond when Adria wasn't around.

"Some girls in line were talking about the site," I said as I set my tray down and took the seat across from them.

"Shhh," Adria urged. "Remember?"

She scanned the area. There were people all around us, but nobody seemed to be paying attention to what we were saying. It was so loud in there, I doubted they could hear us anyway.

"Who?" Janelle asked.

"That Susannah girl from the yearbook staff," I said. "I

don't know the name of her friend for sure. I think it's Trish or Trisha or something like that."

"Doesn't matter," Adria said. "What did they say?"

I quickly reviewed in my mind everything I'd heard and picked out the thing that was most important to share. They didn't need to know all the stuff the girls had said about Damen. He was just a couple of tables away, and I wasn't 100 percent sure my friends wouldn't tell him what the other girls had said.

"It'll probably expand to other kids soon," I said. "All the popular kids will have a page."

I looked to my left and right to indicate the people on either side of us. Every single one of these people could have a page by the end of the week, for all we knew. It wouldn't surprise me.

"We were actually talking about that," Adria said.

"We think we can get the whole thing taken down," Janelle said, leaning forward so she could speak quietly. "It's gossipy. The principal would probably love to know all about it."

So *that* was what they'd been talking about when I

walked up. I felt a little better that the whispering hadn't been intended to leave me out, but to keep anyone else around them from overhearing.

"If the people posting slams found out we were the ones who told, we'd be the most hated people in school," I pointed out.

"Yeah, but they won't find out," Janelle said. "We're not going to actually walk into the principal's office and tell him."

"We're going to send him a link," Adria said, her eyes seeming to twinkle in her excitement. "Anonymously."

"We just have to figure out how to hide our email address," Janelle said, looking down at her phone screen. "Maybe a fake email account or something."

Yeah, I kind of knew the perfect person to ask about that. She just happened to be seated across from them. *Me.* But the thing was, my friends didn't exactly know about my coding club. They knew I liked to develop applications for fun sometimes, but they had no idea just how into it I was. I'd been obsessed with coding since we'd made a fun game in computer class in second grade. It was supposed to be a one-day exercise, but it had stayed with me. Janelle and

Adria had assumed it was something I'd done once for a class project or something, and I never corrected them.

I know, weird. I was just so eager for their approval in the beginning that I hadn't wanted to say something that might make me seem less cool. Even though coding *was* cool in my world. I still to this day had no idea whether it was cool in *their* world.

I would tell them someday. Maybe. If they ever stopped talking long enough to listen.

"If we don't do something, you two will be next," Janelle said, shaking her head. "You're my friends, so it's only natural that someone will think of you. We have to stop SlamBook now."

We had to stop them before they could post anything mean about her. That's what she really meant. And Adria didn't like to hear anything bad about herself. If she asked how she looked, we all knew there was only one answer: great.

There was only one answer I could give now.

"Sure," I said. "We'll figure it out."

CHAPTER 3

Janelle's house was off-the-charts nice. "The kind of house you see on *Real Housewives*" nice. That was one of the best things about being her friend—well, that and the fact that she had one of those pools the size you see when you stay at hotels. There was no better time to be Janelle's BFF than during summer vacation.

But today we were in Janelle's overdecorated bedroom. If Barbie's Dreamhouse was life-size, this was what it would look like. Lots and lots and lots of pink. I sat on top of Janelle's pink polka-dot bedspread with my phone in hand, the SlamBook page open on my screen.

"This wasn't designed by someone our age," I blurted.

I realized that Janelle and Adria were staring at me. I'd said too much. Now wasn't the time to explain that I'd spent the last six months designing a homework helper app.

"What do you mean?" Adria asked.

"How do you know?" Janelle asked, speaking over Adria.

"Well . . ."

The truth was, if a kid our age had designed it, it would have been mobile responsive, at the very least. But if someone our age had done this, it would have been an app. Websites were for businesses and people who didn't know how to design an app.

"Slam books were a thing way back in the fifties," I said instead, suddenly grateful that I'd Wikipedia'd slam books when I was bored during fifth period. "Like, your parents' parents were doing slam books in spiral notebooks and stuff."

"But why would some old person set up a SlamBook site for our school?" Janelle asked. "That makes no sense."

"Maybe it's a test," Adria said. "Like, maybe they're doing some kind of experiment on us. We'll end up in a documentary on middle schoolers today and how we're gossipy or something."

"An email to the principal would make us pass that test," Janelle pointed out. "All the more reason to send it."

Fine. I had no problem coming up with a fake email address. They could have done it themselves, but even without knowing I had a coding background, they were aware that I was better with the tech stuff than they were.

In about thirty seconds, I used Janelle's laptop to set up a burner email account, telling them the account was untraceable. Of course, someone who was supersmart could probably trace the email back to the IP address of Janelle's laptop, but I doubted the principal would go to all that trouble. The email was just going to say that Slam-Book should be taken down anyway, so it wasn't like Janelle could get in trouble for that. She just didn't want our class-mates to know she'd been the one to complain.

"It's up to you to decide what to say," I said, handing the laptop over to Janelle and Adria. Writing anonymous emails to principals was definitely not my thing. Even a short book report felt like some kind of torture.

"Sure," Janelle said. But she didn't *sound* sure. She was

biting her thumbnail, which was something she did when she was nervous.

She just stared at the screen. Adria leaned over to look at it after a few awkward minutes. I wondered if I should suggest a few words to get her started.

"I want some yogurt," Janelle suddenly said, swinging her legs over the side of the bed and standing up. "Anyone want snacks?"

"No, thanks," I said, staring at my phone screen.

"I'll go with you," Adria said, not even looking back at me as she scooted off the bed and rushed after Janelle.

I looked up, my smartphone screen forgotten as the usual insecurities washed over me. Why did Adria really want to go with her? Neither one of them were all that snacky, so I didn't really buy that they were headed out on some sort of junk-food-finding expedition.

Yet another time when I was pushed out of their friendship.

Yeah, that was a little paranoid, I realized. But that was what I thought every time they wandered off without me. I just didn't like feeling left out.

But as I was stressing about that, I saw Janelle's laptop

in my peripheral vision. The computer was all mine, at least until the two of them returned. And they wouldn't return quietly. I could get a look at what was going on with SlamBook while they munched and gossiped in the kitchen.

Janelle had left her own SlamBook page up on the screen. I wondered if she'd memorized all the things people had written about her. I shook my head and scrolled to the bottom of the page. I found what I was looking for in a matter of seconds.

SlamBook, Inc., the fine print said. The words were linked, so I clicked, and went to a main page inviting me to *create a slam book for your school.* This changed things. No longer did it have to be someone with website design knowledge who had set up the Gladesville Middle School slam book. Anyone, anywhere could have set up a Slam-Book site for our school and begun creating pages for our most popular students.

Sighing, I hit the back button and stared at the screen. Janelle was logged in. I thought for a second and shrugged, before logging her out and clicking the link to create a new account. Even if Janelle and Adria came back and saw that

I'd logged her out, who cared? I wasn't sneaking around anymore. I was creating an account of my own so that I could use SlamBook like everyone else in our school was going to use it.

Creating a username and password was the easy part. I gave the name "Sandy," which was what my father had called me when I was younger, because of my sandy-blond hair, and then I used my usual ridiculously long password. I doubted that whoever was running our school site was smart enough to track the account back to me.

That was when things got hard, though. When I hit submit, I had to fill out a long application. My eyes widened as I scrolled down the page. I should have waited until I was home to do all this. I only hoped it would save. They wanted to know what grade I was in, what extracurriculars I did, what part of town I lived in. . . . It was all just too impossible without giving away who I really was.

What would happen if I lied? I wondered.

When I heard Janelle and Adria laughing their way up the stairs to where I was, I froze. My first thought was that I should toss the laptop onto the bed and pretend I'd been just sitting there, quietly waiting for them to return. But then I reminded myself there was no point in that. I was doing nothing wrong.

"I need your help," I said as they came through the door.

Janelle, in particular, would like that. She loved having people ask for advice. Especially when it came to appearancey-type things like what to wear to the movies or whether one selfie looked better than another.

"These questions," I said. "They're just ridic."

"Yep," Janelle said. "And if you don't answer them the right way, the administrators will supposedly reject you."

I had a feeling that was the case. This wasn't just an application. It was a test. If I failed it, I'd probably have to come up with a new username and password, which would just confuse me.

"So how do I answer?"

Janelle breezed over and flopped down onto the bed next to me. I wasn't sure where Adria had gone. I would've sworn I'd heard her voice just seconds before, but she hadn't followed Janelle into the room.

"That's the easy stuff," Janelle said, pointing at what was visible on the screen. It was mostly questions about what grade I was in and who my friends were. I could answer easily if I were being honest.

"Will saying I'm your friend mark me as part of the popular group or something?" I asked. Like there was some kind of "popular alert" set on this page. Doubtful.

She gave me a confused look. "Why would it do that?"

That was another thing about Janelle. She didn't seem to see herself as better than anyone else. Sure, she knew she was well liked, but she didn't let it go to her head like some people would.

"I mean, they may be going after the popular girls in each class. Not that I'm popular at all or anything. But just . . . saying I'm your friend might make whoever's controlling this thing think I am."

Now I was rambling. The good news was, she just rolled her eyes and returned her attention to the page.

"Say you're Tierra's friend," she said, taking over the laptop and typing the words in herself. "Let's see what they do with that. It'll be fun."

I couldn't imagine what they'd do with that and why whatever they did would be "fun." But Janelle was in control. If she wanted to fill in the rest of the fields in the form, I'd be fine with it.

"Extracurriculars," Janelle said, tapping her finger on the *K* key as she thought. "I've got it. Bird-watching and ninja warrior training."

She actually typed those two things in.

"They'll know it's fake if you put that in there," I said. "Make up something more realistic. 'I'm on the yearbook staff and in band' or something."

I was neither. My only extracurricular was the coding club, and it wasn't even a school thing. Each student in the club met with an online mentor once a week to get one-on-one guidance for specific projects. Even if I wanted to tell my friends about it, it didn't count for the slam book since it was something my parents paid for me to do. The school had nothing at all to do with it.

"Perfect," Janelle said. "That sounds just like stuff Tierra would like."

Tierra wasn't really a joiner. She had a new group of people she hung out with, but I didn't know anything about them. Nobody seemed to pay much attention to them, that

I could tell. But I had a feeling everyone was going to be noticing all of them a little more now, thanks to SlamBook. We'd all be looking around, wondering who was writing whatever on various pages.

"That's perfect," I said as Janelle filled out the rest of the fields. Pretend-me lived in a typical neighborhood near the school, going to the movies was my favorite pastime, and I most feared failing algebra. "They'll see me as the very type of person who will criticize *you*."

Janelle stopped typing and turned to look at me. "What did you just say?"

I realized that my words hadn't come out quite the way I'd intended. I immediately backtracked.

"We're your audience," I said. "You get more attention than people like pretend-me."

Or real me. Or even real Adria. But Janelle just shrugged it all off.

"You'd better not be writing something bad about me," she said.

But she had a half smile. I knew she thought that the only thing I'd do with my new pretend account was write nice things about her. She was wrong about that. I was going to use my new account to learn as much as possible about SlamBook so I could figure out what to do next.

"I'm going to write something on your page," I said, reaching for her laptop.

She sat back, grabbing her smartphone and staring at the door.

"Adria!" she called toward the empty doorway. "Where'd you go?"

No answer. Janelle went straight to her phone, and I knew she was texting Adria. Which was great for me, since it meant I had time to figure out what I was going to write.

I could think of all the things I'd say about her, but this wasn't about me. It was about pretend-me. What would the average person wandering the hallways at school say about her? Probably that she was snobby or something. I wasn't an idiot. I knew that even though Janelle made every effort to be nice to everyone she met throughout the day, she could only talk to a small percentage of the whole school. And people could be secretly mean about cheerleaders, as I'd noticed before I'd started hanging out with one.

It wasn't too hard to think up something to say, actually, mostly because I always felt like I was seconds away from not being part of Janelle's circle anymore. I took a deep breath and typed a few words.

Supersweet and sooooo adorable, I wrote. Then, without asking for Janelle's permission, I pressed the post button.

Only after I was staring at my words, live on the screen, did I realize what I'd done. First of all, I wasn't even sure I'd been approved yet, but my post had gone through. Which was just weird, considering all the questions I'd had to answer.

"'Sup?" Adria said as she breezed through the door, carrot stick hanging out of her mouth.

"Faith is leaving a comment for me," Janelle said.

"Cool," Adria said. "You should say she's the best dresser in school. What? You are."

Janelle was staring at Adria. Or maybe it was a glare. I couldn't tell for sure. But I had to break it to both of them that I'd already written something.

"It's live," I said, pointing at the screen while bracing myself for them to want me to change what I'd said. Could we even edit comments after we'd posted them? I had a feeling that was a hard *no*.

Adria and Janelle leaned forward to look at the screen. Janelle squinted at it. Then a smile slowly started to spread across her face. She liked it. I let out the breath I hadn't even realized I'd been holding.

"Ugh," Adria said.

The smile on Janelle's face promptly vanished. She looked at me, then turned to Adria.

"What?" both Janelle and I asked in unison.

"It's just so . . . *repetitive*," Adria said, rolling her eyes. "The other comments were pretty much the same thing. Can't you be original?"

Rude. I hadn't had much time to think. If Adria was so smart, why didn't she create an account and write something? I looked at the screen, hoping suddenly that an option to edit had appeared on the page since the last time I'd looked.

Nope.

"Okay, so your turn," Janelle said, turning the laptop to face Adria. "Create an account and write something not-repetitive about me."

That was another reason why I liked Janelle so much. She didn't have to kiss anyone's butt, so she didn't. If someone like Adria needed to be checked, Janelle checked her. But that didn't stop her from being nice to everyone. She just handled everything in such a calm, mature manner. Everyone needed a friend like Janelle.

"I don't really want an account," Adria said. "If I get an account, next thing I know, I'll have a page and people will be writing stuff about me."

"That's not how it works," Janelle said.

"Oh really? How do you know? Do you really know for sure?"

Adria had a point. We didn't know how any of this worked. We didn't even know that whoever had set up the page for our school couldn't somehow figure out who I really was through the fake account I'd made. Maybe the camera on Janelle's laptop had secretly snapped a picture of me or something. The thought gave me chills.

"Janelle can help you set up a fake account," I said. "Pretend name and everything. She even answered the questions in a way that would throw the administrators off. They probably think I hang out with Tierra or something."

My own words gave me a pang of guilt that I'd thrown Tierra's name out there like that. She'd been good to me, and I was trying to fit in at her expense. I was a horrible, horrible person.

"Oh," Adria said. Chewing on her lip, she stared at the laptop. She was considering it, I could tell. Finally she said, "Okay."

The two of them got to work setting up Adria's account, and I scooted up near the bed's headboard, so I could use my smartphone without risk of anyone seeing the screen. I couldn't stay away from SlamBook.

I couldn't really dig deep into the code behind the site on my phone, so I opted for just bouncing around, checking out various pages. The exercise was meant to be something to help me learn all of it better so that I could crack into it and figure out who was running everything. Who had set this up? Why? I knew this couldn't end well. But in the meantime, *wowzers.*

If I had a face like hers, I'd sue my parents.

The 1900s called. They want their hairstyle back.

So vapid that I'm surprised her empty head hasn't caved in.

I rolled my eyes at the comments about people's looks. Speaking of vapid . . . I told myself that if a page ever appeared with my name at the top, I just needed to remember what I was thinking right now, which was that attacking someone's looks was completely unoriginal. It was what someone said when they couldn't think of anything intelligent to say. That kind of comment said more about the people posting the comments than the person they were talking about. Of course, none of us knew who the commenters were, since it was all anonymous, so it didn't hurt those who were writing mean things anyway, I supposed. Commenting about people's looks was just so, so eyeroll-worthy.

As I scrolled past all the shallow attacks on people's faces, butts, and noses, something caught my eye. It was a comment that hit me so hard, it made my fingers freeze on the trackpad.

Who? I don't even know who this person is, she's such a nobody.

I scrolled to the top of the page to look at the person's name. I didn't recognize it. I told myself that was probably because the person was in a different grade, but I wasn't so sure about that, honestly. It very well could be that she was one of the watchers I was thinking about. The people who stayed in the background, living their lives just fine but not getting noticed by most of their fellow students.

If I was honest, I was 99 percent sure I was just like them. *If* I was even on anyone's radar, it was as "Janelle's friend." Or, more likely, "That girl who always follows Janelle around like a lost puppy dog."

I didn't need anyone to use SlamBook to slam me. I could do just fine with my own insults.

Sighing, I set my phone down. The comments on those pages may have been oddly addictive to read through, but they'd messed with my mind. In a seriously bad way. I looked at Janelle and Adria, giggling over whatever silly answer they'd just put into the registration form. If it made friends get together and have fun like this, SlamBook could be a good thing, but I had a feeling the website would be far from that. It would mostly be students sitting home alone, refreshing the SlamBook page to see if anything new had been posted about them. And if someone got twenty positive comments and one negative, the negative would be the only thing that stood out.

"Fly fishing?" Adria said. "Or . . . I know . . . glow golf."

"I think it has to be something our school actually offers," I said. Not that I was an expert on SlamBook or anything. I didn't want it to sound that way. I started to try to think up something to say to make it clear that I had no idea what I was talking about, but then I realized the two of them weren't listening to me. I might as well not even have been sitting there.

I was the third wheel, yet again.

My phone buzzed in my hand, immediately pulling my attention back to the screen. A notification from Slam-Book. I didn't even know I'd signed up for notifications. Probably some little box I'd left checked somewhere. But the text of the notification actually made me less annoyed about that.

JazzyB liked your slam, it read.

That was followed by another buzz. Then another. I clicked on one of them, and it took me to Janelle's page. Sure enough, there was a tiny heart by my comment with the number three next to it. That jumped to four, then five, fortunately not accompanied by a notification. The website developer must have set SlamBook to only notify on the first three notifications or something. Interesting choice. I would have chosen to stop after one. I wondered if they'd also time-delayed it so that if there were no likes for eight hours or something, the site notified me the next time one came in.

Five people liked my slam. Which was a made-up slam that was super nice. I clicked over to a page with mean slams and noted that they had a ridiculous number of likes. In the three figures, actually. One even had a tiny blue ribbon next to it. I had no idea what that meant. It had won a prize or something?

I thought about Damen King. I didn't know much about him, but I remembered the convo I'd overheard in the lunch line and that the girls had said he was full of himself. Also, that he had a page.

I did a search for his name and the page popped up. Man, they weren't kidding. His slams made the worst ones I'd seen look like compliments. For some reason, though, I had a feeling someone like him wouldn't even be upset at the things people were saying. If he was full of himself, nothing anyone could say would get through that big ego, right?

Somehow, that thought gave me confidence. I could write anything about him, and he wouldn't care. I closed my eyes and pictured the guy I'd seen strutting around the halls of school, big smirk on his face, looking around to see who was staring at him. I couldn't say for 100 percent sure he'd been doing that when I'd seen him, but it seemed right.

To leave a comment about him, I just had to click a button and automatically a field would pop up. In that little box, I typed the most creative insult I could think of.

CHAPTER 4

"What's a 'roid head?"

My question made Mom choke on her water. It made Dad freeze, forkful of quinoa just inches from his face. And it made Hope's mouth drop open. Luckily, there was no food in it.

"What?" I asked.

"What did you say?" Mom asked.

"No . . . wait . . . don't say it again," Dad said. He was shaking his head, like it was something bad. I was thinking maybe it had something to do with robots or something— as in, someone who has an empty head like a robot.

"Steroids?" Hope asked. "*Hello?* You've never heard of steroids?"

"*You* have?" Mom asked Hope. She looked seriously flummoxed.

"Well, yeah," Hope said, but from the look on her face, I could tell she'd realized that speaking up may not have been the wisest of choices. "I mean, I watch Netflix."

I nodded, returning my attention to dinner. That made sense. I didn't really watch much TV. I spent my nights either studying or working on my app. On the weekends, sometimes I'd veg on my bed with my laptop and a bunch of shows, but nothing that talked about steroids.

"So, what?" I asked. "Steroids make your head empty or something?"

"I don't know," Dad said. "I'm just guessing it refers to someone who does steroids too much. Why are you asking?"

"Where did you hear this?" Mom asked.

Oops. The last thing I wanted to do was tell the 'rents about SlamBook. They'd blow a gasket, for sure.

"I just heard someone say it today," I said, shrugging. "At school."

I supposed someone could argue that I hadn't technically lied. Whoever had written those words on Damen King's SlamBook page was from school. And I'd read it earlier today, which was kind of like hearing it. Yeah, it was a lie, for sure.

"Whoever said that must be a very insecure person," Mom said, returning her attention to her plate.

"How so?" I asked.

"Insecure people talk about other people," Hope jumped in to explain. "It's how they make themselves feel better."

Hope was the Janelle of her grade. Always had been. So basically, I'd gone from living in the shadow of my big sister to living in the shadow of Janelle. But it felt like a step up to be the popular girl's friend rather than the ignored little sister of the popular girl, as I'd always been with Hope.

"Very astute, Hope," Dad said. Then he turned toward me. "This wasn't a friend of yours or anything. Not Janelle."

"Janelle's such a nice girl," Mom said.

"Seems more like something Adria would say," Hope said with a shrug.

"Hope!" Mom said.

"Sorry," Hope said.

But it was fine, because Hope had big news. She was going to regionals with her cheer squad. Oh, and also, her painting was going to be on display at the art show in November. Oh, and also, she was getting all A-plus-pluses on her report card or whatever. I had to hold myself back from rolling my eyes because that would have been so rude.

As expected, the rest of the dinner conversation was all about art shows and cheer competitions. Which was fine, since I had a videoconference with Ms. Wang, my coding mentor, at seven and I really needed to pull up my work for the past few days and look over it. Ms. Wang coded apps for the government during the day and worked with students like me at night. I just told her my progress and she helped me with any areas where I was stuck. My coding work was so much easier during the week when I knew that if I had any problems, I could just wait until I talked to her to get unstuck.

"May I please be excused?" I asked after putting serious effort into shoving the rest of the food on my plate into my mouth. Nobody even noticed how quickly I was eating. No surprise.

"That wasn't part of the agreement," Dad was saying to Hope.

"You said you'd pay for my uniforms if I paid for gymnastics," Hope said. "And I won't have time to keep up with my chores."

"How so?" Dad asked.

Hope sighed and set down her fork. "I have to double up on practice, since I'm doing both football and basketball. Then there's schoolwork and—"

"None of that should interfere with your chores," Dad said. "You can do them all on weekends."

"Cheerleading is important, though," Mom said.

"So are her chores," Dad argued.

"But the better she is, the better her chances of a college scholarship someday," Mom pointed out. "Free money."

"Excuse me?" I asked. "I really need to—"

The word "go" disappeared as my father gave his stern, "These kids need to learn responsibility" lecture to my mom. Although it was really directed at Hope, who was

 60

now staring at her fingernails, bored. Meanwhile, I had better things to do.

Fine. If they weren't going to acknowledge me, I'd get up and they wouldn't be able to help themselves. The second I stood up, I'd get a lecture about how we stayed at the table until dinner was finished, young lady, or we at least asked for permission. I'd point out that I *had* asked for permission, only nobody had been paying a bit of attention to me.

I stood and took my plate to the sink. They kept talking. I even rinsed my plate off and put it into the dishwasher—making as much noise as possible—and still, they kept talking. I turned and looked at them. Hope was the only one who seemed to notice me. She gave me a *Help me* look, and I was pretty sure she was going to rat me out. But she just sat there, her eyes narrowing as I flounced out of the room. I wondered if they'd even notice I was gone when it was time to clean up.

Once I was in front of my laptop, I forgot all about that. I scooted around until my bulletin board was behind me, as I always did, since that was the most work-like thing in my room. I certainly didn't want Ms. Wang to see my stuffed-animal corner or the Polaroids of me, Janelle, and Adria being silly over the summer.

Trying to shut out everything but thoughts of my homework helper app, I pulled up my app builder and went back over the work I'd been doing earlier that morning. I was stuck. There was no way around it. I needed Ms. Wang's help.

Because I didn't want to lose the screen I had open, I grabbed the Post-it pad next to my computer and scrawled out some notes. Just a few questions I wanted to ask Ms. Wang. I knew things could get a little chitchatty at the start, and I didn't want to forget what I'd planned to ask. It would suck if I got off the videoconference and found myself sitting there, with days ahead of me, and no way to get the answers I needed.

Yeah, I could email her and ask any questions at any time, but she was super busy, so this was always best.

My computer started bing-bonging long before I expected it to. I was sure she was early, until I looked up at the top right corner of my screen. Seven-oh-two. Hadn't it just been six o'clock or something? *Sheesh.*

I pressed the answer button, and Ms. Wang's smiling face filled the screen. Ms. Wang was *the best* tutor ever, anywhere. If I could replace all my teachers with her and just have her teach everything for the rest of my life, I'd be fine with that.

"What up?" Ms. Wang said.

So . . . yeah. Sometimes she tried to sound younger than she was. From anyone else, that would have been annoying, but from her it somehow worked.

"Not much," I said.

So much. So, so, *so* much. I wanted to tell her all about SlamBook and how off balance the day had been, but something stopped me. I knew Ms. Wang would get such a kick out of the way-outdated design of the site and the fact that it was a site in the first place, rather than being an app, like it should have been. She could have helped me figure out who was controlling things and maybe even crack the code to figure out who was posting what.

But she also could pick up the phone and call the school. Or send an email to the principal. Heck, she could probably even call someone and have it on the evening news.

I did not want that. Not yet, anyway. I wanted to work on this myself for a while, and if SlamBook was busted, I couldn't do that.

"You know I live vicariously through you guys," she said with a big smile. "All day in an office with a bunch of people seated in front of computers. Nobody even talks. Everyone just has earbuds in their ears, fingers on the keyboard."

Considering she was seated in front of her computer with earbuds in her ears at that very moment, that was a little funny. But I didn't point that out.

"Yeah, well, middle school is basically the same without the earbuds," I said. "Or the computers. Just kids sitting at desks, frantically scribbling notes."

"But you have all that chatty time between classes," she said. "I'm young enough to remember that. The rumors. The giggling. The *gossip*."

"Aren't gossip and rumors the same thing?" I asked.

"I guess so," she said. "Either way, both are bad."

She was right about that, and suddenly I felt really, really guilty. I'd gotten way too caught up in reading mean things people were saying about each other. Not to mention the thrill I'd felt while reading the notifications of all the people who'd liked my comment about Damen—that he was a dork pretending to be cool. Every buzz made me smile a little more. It made me feel liked. And my comment didn't have nearly as many likes as the "'roid head" one from a couple of hours ago.

It was all just wrong. Very, very wrong. I knew it, yet I'd done it anyway.

"I think I'd rather do what you do," I said. "Just sit at a computer all day, writing code. That would be so much fun."

She laughed. "Yeah, about that . . . You know that feeling you have when you get stuck?"

"Yes."

"That's me every day so far this week," she said. "You work and work, and when you're ready to test what you've done, it's just broken. I know you know that feeling."

Yep. That was pretty much always the feeling I had when I was coding. I'd done some super-simple apps in the early days because that was how coding classes started you out. But now I was shooting for the big leagues. I had someone to help me get unstuck, but I wanted to do it on my own. I wanted to figure it out somehow.

"Have you uploaded your latest?" she asked.

The upload. I'd forgotten to share my document. That was the most important part of this get-together. I'd been so distracted with everything else going on, I'd gotten out of my routine.

"Uploading now," I said. "I'm just a little stuck. Okay, a *lot* stuck. I'm hoping you can help me work it out."

"I'll take a look," she said. "Hey, anything new with your friend Janelle?"

I'd told Ms. Wang all about Janelle. I should have mentioned Adria, too, but I had a bad habit of underplaying her. In other words, when I talked about my friends to people like Ms. Wang or my parents' friends or my hairstylist, I made it sound like it was Janelle and me, BFFs, and everyone else was just secondary.

I tried to dig through recent Janelle news, but the number one biggest thing in Janelle's life right now was that there was a page on the internet with her name on top. And I couldn't tell Ms. Wang about that.

"She's all worried about some gossip," I said, which was sort of telling Ms. Wang about SlamBook, but not really.

Gossip was gossip, whether it was on a website or in person, right?

"Gossip?" Ms. Wang asked.

"Yeah, apparently people are saying nice things about her."

"I hate it when that happens," Ms. Wang said, rolling her eyes.

"Exactly!" I said. "There can be worse things than people saying you're sweet and pretty."

Ms. Wang thought about it a second. "I don't know," she said. "I think it can be a little unsettling to know people are talking about you, even if it's nice."

Yes, I'd thought about that too. Janelle had pretty much said as much. Hadn't she even called SlamBook creepy? But people talked about other people. That's what they did. Now it had just been put on a website, for all the world to see.

"So what did Janelle do?"

"About what?" I asked. I was having a hard time following Ms. Wang's train of thought.

"The gossip."

"Oh," I said. "She's a little creeped out, but she'll get over it. As long as they don't start saying bad things about her."

"There's a saying," Ms. Wang said. "'What someone else thinks of me is none of my business.' I think those are some pretty good words to live by, don't you?"

Wow. Ms. Wang was there to help me with my app. But as I watched her go through my code while I frantically took notes, I realized she was helping me with so much more than that. Somehow, she'd managed to make me feel better about SlamBook. Even if someone said bad things about me or Janelle or anyone else, it was just one person's opinion. And really, who cared what one person thought?

"You're not going to believe this," Ms. Wang said, her fingers flying over the keyboard. She had a big smile on her face that jumped out at me through the screen. "Just a simple fix. I've sent you the line of code, but read it over and let me know if you have any questions before we disconnect."

I didn't want to disconnect, I realized as I opened the file and saw the small mistake I'd made. This was an easy fix. I could move forward with my app. I should have been jumping up and down in my chair with excitement.

Instead I had this weird, sinking feeling that my conversation with Ms. Wang had been super disappointing, and I didn't really know why. Except the fact that Ms. Wang has asked specifically about Janelle when she should have been asking how things were going with *me*.

How many weeks had it been like that? How many weeks had I just worked on my app and hung out with my friends and had nothing really all that interesting to say about my life?

When was I going to start living *my* story instead of Janelle's?

CHAPTER 5

Riding the bus sucked. But that was what happened when I hardly slept because I'd been checking my phone for SlamBook notifications throughout the night. By the time I'd finally dragged myself out of bed and shoved some clothes on, Mom had already called my name seven or eight times—I'd lost count.

Riding the bus also meant I got to school later than if Dad drove me. Which meant I rushed through the door and straight to my locker with only a few minutes to spare before the first warning bell. No biggie, but I was a little annoyed that I'd missed breakfast. No sleep, no food . . .

By about nine thirty I'd be feeling pretty weak. I wondered if there was time to get a granola bar out of the vending machine before homeroom.

My phone buzzed in my back pocket as I was pulling my first-period books out of my locker. Maybe a granola bar between homeroom and first period. If I didn't have to swing by my locker between first and second, I could grab some extra minutes at some point.

I pulled my phone out of my pocket and read the text. **Where R U?** Janelle had written.

No time to answer. I shoved my phone into my pocket, grabbed my second-period stuff, and slammed my locker door shut. Janelle was in my homeroom, so I'd see her in, like, two minutes anyway.

But as I took off toward homeroom, my phone buzzed again. And again. And again. Sighing, I pulled it out and looked at the screen. More texts from Janelle, and now a call was coming in.

We never, ever called each other.

"Hey," I said into the phone as I race-walked toward homeroom.

"Why aren't you here?" Janelle asked. "I've been texting."

She'd been texting for all of three minutes. Not very patient. Which wasn't like Janelle. Usually she texted once and went on with her life. You got back to her when you got back to her. There had to be a reason why she was being so *not* chill today.

"I'm walking into homeroom now," I said.

Janelle spotted me and tapped her screen to hang up. "Hurry," she whispered, motioning for me to come closer. I plopped down in my seat, but not without first noticing the absence of one very enthusiastic Amy Tatem.

"Before Amy gets here," she said. "Have you checked the page this morning?"

I could honestly say no, unless three a.m. counted as "this morning." It had been just after three when I'd last checked the page before finally drifting off to sleep. But even then, I hadn't been checking Janelle's page, which I was pretty sure she was referring to. I'd been checking the area that listed the people who'd recently had pages created, which still had Janelle's name, along with a bunch of others. I felt like all of a sudden some new names would appear there. Not mine, but maybe someone like Adria or

 72

a dozen or so other popular kids who were on my radar.

"You're there," she whispered. "Adria, too. But your pages are blank so far."

"Blank?" I whispered.

That was far, far worse than not having a page at all. To have a SlamBook page and have nobody even care enough to write one thing about me? That was all kinds of ick.

"Do you think the page will be taken down if nobody posts there?" I asked.

Janelle shrugged. "There were a bunch of new pages this morning when I checked it. Probably just popped up. There hasn't been time for people to post. Give it until later tonight. You'll see. Here comes Amy."

"Ohmigosh, you guys, did you hear?" she asked *way* loudly.

I winced. Out of the corner of my eye, I saw Janelle squirm in her seat. She was looking around, no doubt checking to see if anyone was listening.

"There's this SlamBook thingy, and you're both on it!" she squealed.

Again, wincing.

"Shhh," Janelle urged. She looked around.

Amy looked around too. "Oh, come on. Everyone knows. You all know about SlamBook, right?" she asked the people next to us.

A couple of people nodded. The rest just looked at her like she was either mildly annoying or completely off her rocker. My vote was for her being a combination of both.

"Just sit," Janelle said, but when she said it, she made it sound charming rather than rude.

I got it. Amy didn't. It wasn't that people didn't know about SlamBook or we were trying to keep it a secret or something. It was that Janelle didn't want anyone to know she was involved in a convo about it. That would make it seem like (a) she was aware of the site's existence, and, *worse*, (b) she actually cared about it.

"Okay," Amy said, sliding into her seat and finally lowering her voice to a whisper. "So, they're saying some awesome stuff about you, Janelle." She looked at me. "You don't have anything yet, but I'm going to register and post something super nice. Let's keep it going."

If anyone posted anything at all about me, I'd be happy about it. Heck, what was I thinking? I could post something about me. I had that fake log-in and all. But what if the person administering the site traced my IP address and somehow figured out I was posting to my own page?

No, silly. The site could have been set up by someone way far away, for all we knew. Someone else had just created a page for our school. That person would probably not have any more power to see who posted what than I would. Probably much less.

"I already posted something nice about you," Amy told Janelle. "The 'smile brighter than the sun' comment? All me!"

She was quite proud of that, but I hadn't seen that one. Maybe it was new. Or maybe it blended in with all the nicey-nice comments about Janelle's looks. I knew Janelle. She was flattered by the looks stuff, but it was far more important to her to be appreciated for her smarts and personality.

"I can't believe Mr. Marquez hasn't done something about it," Amy said. "I'm sure he doesn't know it exists. He can't know. Right?"

I looked at Janelle. We'd set up the fake email account, but we'd gotten distracted before sending an actual email to the principal. I hoped she'd forgotten about it, at least until I could figure out what was going on.

But by lunchtime it had become clear that there was no escaping talk of SlamBook. Everyone, in every class, was sneaking peeks at their phones, checking to see if there were any updates. Then they'd share the posts with everyone around them. If Mr. Marquez didn't know about it yet, he would by the end of the day. Any second now, someone would be caught violating the "no cell phone" policy and a teacher would find out about SlamBook and pass the info on to the boss.

"Skinny fat," Adria said. "Someone actually called me skinny fat. What is that even?"

"Skinny but out of shape," Janelle said, holding up her phone to show that she'd looked it up.

"Like, you don't live in a gym or something," I said. "Probably someone who does nothing but exercise. Maybe Damen King wrote it."

Both Adria and Janelle were staring at me by then, and I realized I'd slipped up. Why had I said that?

"Damen King?" Janelle asked.

"What do you know?" Adria asked. "Did he say something about me?"

"No, but his SlamBook has something about it," I said. "All he does is work out, right?"

Janelle and Adria looked at each other, then looked at me again. "He's in good shape, I guess," Janelle said. "I just thought it was from football."

"Look at the slams for him," I said, hoping that would be enough to get me out of the conversation. Because honestly, I didn't want them to know just how much I'd been watching the slam book site since finding out about it. We all three looked over at Damen, who was standing at the end of the jock table, talking to someone. I didn't want to repeat any of the slams I'd seen. I'd said enough.

"I don't think they should attack appearance," I commented.

"Agreed," Janelle said. "And that's the stuff that makes me want to report it to Mr. Marquez. It's not fun when people get hurt."

Janelle was right. This was all kinds of wrong. I didn't like what it was doing to me, and I didn't like that it was hurting people. All we had to do was send an email, and the school administration would surely have the Gladesville Middle School slam book taken down. Even if we didn't do anything, though, it was only a matter of time before somebody's parent or one of the teachers found out about Slam-Book and threw a fit over it.

And life would go back to what it had been. I would work on my app, and Janelle and Adria would continue bonding over things I would never really be interested in—like the perfect smoky eye and nail art.

There was something about the lure of SlamBook. Just knowing that I could go to the site right then on my phone and read what everyone was saying about everyone else . . . It wasn't really an adventure, but it fed into some part of me that was just—well, *nosy*.

"What are they saying about you?" Janelle asked me.

The question threw me off guard. I really had no idea. Did I want to know? I was afraid to know. But I *had* to know.

French fry in one hand and phone in the other, I woke up my phone and hit the back button on the browser until I got to the page on me. Then I refreshed, and, sure enough, there was one comment. One. But at least it was something.

"Don't know her," I read.

Silence from my friends. Really? Just . . . really? Some-one had felt the need to write that? Why bother?

But then I reminded myself that this was the only per-son who had bothered. Everyone else who had seen my name on the list of new pages had scrolled right on by. I was still a total ghost at school, despite being Janelle's friend. What the heck was the point?

"I'll leave a comment for you," Adria offered me. "And you leave one for me."

"Great idea!" Janelle said.

I breathed a sigh of relief. Okay, so yeah, maybe I was still no Janelle, but I did have friends who cared about stuff like SlamBook. Just knowing Adria would help me out made me feel a little better. And it was still early. Maybe once people started seeing my name out there, I'd get more comments?

"Okay," Amy said, plopping down next to me. Out of the blue. Amy had never once sat with us at lunch. She had her prime spot with all the other fashionistas who were popular just for looking like Forever 21 window mannequins.

Janelle and Adria exchanged a look. I wanted to

explain to Adria that this was a continuation of a conversation from homeroom, but she was getting all her unspoken info from Janelle, apparently.

"So, I was thinking . . . ," Amy began. "Everyone's being all shallow and stuff with their slams. We should be better than that."

"Agreed," Janelle said.

This made no sense. "The whole thing is shallow," I pointed out. "Kind of by definition."

"But we can make it not shallow," she said. "For instance, for you, I'm thinking about mentioning that you read every single one of Jane Austen's books over summer vacation."

"Not all of them," I said. "Just the ones in volume one."

My mom had a book that had a bunch of Jane Austen's most popular works all bound together. I'd started reading it for something to do last summer, but I'd soon found I was completely addicted. On the first day of school, when Amy had asked what I'd done over the summer besides hanging out with Janelle and taking yoga, I'd mentioned that. Mostly because I hadn't wanted to tell her that I'd also spent hours every day planning the app I was going to develop for the coding club I'd joined.

"Boring," Adria said, rolling her eyes.

"Not at all," Janelle said. "I think it makes her sound very interesting. Like one of those mysterious women who sit on window seats reading books."

I waited for Adria's smart-aleck retort, but what was I thinking? Of course Adria wouldn't argue. Reading was now the awesomest thing ever because Janelle had said so.

"And, Janelle," Amy said. "Remember that food drive last year? I thought I'd mention something about that. You made seven trips to your mom's car to get all the food you guys collected."

"And you did that Christmas angel thingy," Adria pointed out.

"So . . . What, now we're just listing charitable things we do?" Janelle asked. "I don't think that's what SlamBook is supposed to be."

"But think of what we can make it," Amy said. "So much better than it is."

"It's not going to work," I said.

I didn't like saying it any more than she probably liked hearing it. It wasn't pretty. But no matter how many gushy

81

things or bizarre things or socially-conscious things we tried to put on our pages, nobody would care. The majority of comments would still be about silly things like someone being "skinny fat."

"She's right," Janelle said. "You can't polish a turd."

I nearly choked on the sip of bottled water I'd taken. Amy and Adria were both staring at her like she'd just grown a horn and announced she was a unicorn.

"Wait . . . what?" Adria asked.

"It's something my dad always says," Janelle answered with a shrug. "In this case, SlamBook is the turd. You can do whatever you want to pretty it up, but at the end of the day, it's . . . well . . ."

"A turd," I finished for her.

We all laughed. I felt a little better, because maybe everyone felt that way about SlamBook. Especially now that I had a page, even though I obviously wasn't popular enough for people to comment about me.

"I say we just report the site and get it taken down," Janelle said.

"No!" Amy said so loudly that people all around us turned to look at her.

"Apparently Amy is enjoying reading slams a little too much," Adria muttered.

"I'm just . . . I want to see where it goes, right?" Amy asked, looking around.

I got what she was saying, but I was still feeling torn about the whole thing. I knew it was wrong to want to sit back and watch what chaos SlamBook could cause, but if we just tore the whole thing apart now, we'd never know. Wouldn't we regret it? Wouldn't we always wonder?

"They'll just start it back up again," I blurted as soon as the thought hit my brain. "Only this time, they'd be more secretive about it. It would become this underground thing that everyone whispered about. Now that everyone knows the site is out there, it won't just go away."

"Can someone do that?" Janelle asked. "Make another SlamBook if the principal takes this one down?"

I hesitated. I didn't want to give away how much I knew about the site, but it didn't take an app developer to notice that SlamBook wasn't just our school's thing. So I decided to go for it.

"If you click on the logo in the upper right corner, it takes you to a main page," I said. "You can get to your school from there. There are tons of other schools listed on the main page. This is a national thing."

I held my breath while I watched their reaction. Sure, this was something anyone who had ever used a computer could figure out, but the three of them obviously hadn't put it together yet.

"She's right," Amy said. "I saw all the schools there. Didn't you guys start at the main page?"

Okay, maybe someone else had figured it out.

"No," I said. "I saw Janelle's page first."

"Reporting the site wouldn't help, then, I guess," Amy said, sounding a little too happy about that. She was definitely against removing the site.

"Crud," Janelle said, crumpling up her protein bar wrapper and tossing it onto her tray. "So we just have to sit here and watch all this."

"Or not check your page," Adria suggested.

Janelle gave her a look. I could read that look, for sure. Janelle couldn't *not* look at her page. It called her name. She probably told herself she wouldn't look again, but then she'd give in, telling herself she just wanted to take a peek to see if anything new had been posted. I knew the feeling.

I'd known about my page for only a few hours, and I was fighting checking it every second.

"We'll figure something out," Amy said. "But in the meantime, I'm posting some real stuff about the two of you. And you too, if you want, Adria."

Adria smiled, but the smile didn't quite reach her eyes. For once, Adria was the one left out. I knew it was only because Amy was in homeroom with Janelle and me, but it still made me feel like I was somebody for a change.

Amy left and an awkward silence fell between the three of us. Janelle didn't seem to realize anything was up, though. She just started talking without pausing even to take a breath.

"I mean, she's right. You're right. It's— There has to be something we can do. This can't just keep going on. Maybe if we created a fake account and started posting something on every single page about how stupid all of this is. Maybe we could spoil it for everyone and our school's SlamBook would just go away?"

"A bunch of accounts," Adria said. "It would take multiple ones."

"Nah," I said. "The person in charge of things would

85

just go through and delete it all. I'm sure whoever the administrator is has the power to do that."

They both looked at me like I was a little strange. Eventually I was going to have to let them know exactly how much I could help them with SlamBook. We could work together to figure all of this out. After all, if I could get into the code behind SlamBook somehow and discover who was leaving which comments, I'd want to tell someone, right? Someone besides Ms. Wang.

"Um—" I began.

"You guys," Adria interrupted before I could get the words out. She was frowning and looking at her phone again. "Look at this."

We all crowded around her phone. It was a nasty, mean post about how Adria didn't really belong in America. It said that she should go back to her own country. Adria had been born in this country. Had lived in the US her whole life. But her mom was from the Philippines. I'd never heard anyone say a bad word about Adria before, but now SlamBook was bringing all kinds of awfulness out.

We were all silent for a moment. I put my arm around Adria, who looked super upset.

 86

"Oh, it's *on* now," Janelle said quietly. "I don't know what we're going to do, but we're going to do something. We have to."

"I think if the principal found out there was racist stuff—" I began.

"Someone would just start a new page for our school," Adria reminded me. "And this time students would be careful not to post anything racist."

Maybe I could figure out who'd written the horrible things about Adria and use that information to go after them somehow. People wouldn't be so brave if their identities were revealed to everyone, right?

I knew what I had to do. I had to go home, figure out how to crack into the admin section of the SlamBook website, and get log-in information for the people behind these nasty comments. I didn't know what I'd do once I found out, but getting the data was the first step toward doing something to make this situation better. And making my friend feel a little better too.

CHAPTER 6

Hope was at gymnastics. I was at the library. That pretty much summed up the differences between my sister and me.

I set up in the corner, wishing for the ninetieth time that this place had a private area for people with laptops.

Even though I knew people probably couldn't see my screen, today I was especially cautious. Because I was on SlamBook, trying to figure out how the administration of the site worked. Once I did that, I was going to try to guess what the admin password might be.

I'd already figured out, in a matter of seconds, that this

whole thing was just a basic free web design site. Which was no big deal, but it told me that the main SlamBook site hadn't been set up by some huge multinational corporation or something. Likely some bored teen somewhere had set up the page, wanting to mess with people.

And that brought me to the person who had set up our school's slam book on the site. Just one of us, I figured. A middle-school student likely didn't follow the rules for complex passwords, and that meant I could find a way into our school's section as admin if I thought hard enough about it. In fact, I wouldn't have been surprised if there were multiple administrators for our school and they all shared a password. I doubted any of them knew anything about setting up and adminning a website.

I did what anyone with decent tech skills would do. I Googled and hoped it wouldn't make me end up with a virus on my computer or something. I learned everything I needed to know about how the site was set up on the back end. Then I used that information to figure out exactly where I could find the admin log-in for my school's slam book.

Just as I was starting to get somewhere, something in my peripheral vision caught my attention. Tierra. She walked into the library and headed straight to the circulation desk, which was in my line of vision. I slid down in my seat a little. Not that my laptop screen would conceal me completely, but it just felt like I could make myself smaller somehow.

Tierra spoke to the library clerk, who pointed to the right. In the opposite direction from where I was sitting. I breathed a sigh of relief. Crisis averted. As Tierra walked away, I turned my attention back to my website hacking.

In a matter of minutes, I'd figured out how to get the admin log-in info by studying the URL of our school's specific slam book. That was when the real work began. It was never easy to get a password, and it wasn't like I'd ever done this before. But I was learning, and it was for a good cause.

I was so caught up in reading about software that could guess passwords that I didn't see Tierra coming toward me until she was almost to my table. She pulled out a chair, without being invited, and just plopped down across from me.

"So . . . I heard about your page," she said.

I stared at her over the top of my laptop screen for a

long minute. Aside from that morning in front of school, we hadn't talked in, like, forever. Why was she speaking to me all of a sudden?

"You know, the slam thing," she said. "It's . . . Well, I'm sorry. Is there something I can do?"

Okay, now she had my attention. The last time I'd looked at my page, it had just had one comment, which was basically that I was a nobody. I'd checked my page after lunch, but I'd forgotten about it as the afternoon had gone on. My mind had been 100 percent occupied with hacking into the website.

Meanwhile, while I hadn't been paying attention, something had happened?

I didn't want Tierra to know that I had no idea what she was talking about. It was a pride thing, I figured. I forced my expression to remain neutral as I tried to come up with a good answer.

"No, I don't think so," I said. "It's all silly anyway. Just a bunch of trolls trolling. Everyone's all brave when they can hide behind a username, right?"

She tilted her head to the side slightly, and I could see her studying me. It made me nervous. Tierra knew me better than any of my friends. She just always "got" me. I didn't really miss that about her. It was hard to keep secrets from someone who knew you that well.

"You can figure it out, though, I'll bet," she commented. "You always were really good with computers."

Tierra had always been so supportive of my coding stuff. She'd encouraged me to sign up for a class and had been so excited when I'd told her I had a mentor for the summer. Until that very minute in the library, I hadn't realized how much I'd missed having a friend to share that with.

"So far, there's not a page for me," she said. "Hopefully it'll stay that way."

That brought me back down to earth, mostly because I doubted there would ever be a page for Tierra. I was still shocked that there was one for me. Since the first comment for *me* had been from someone who had no idea who I was, I didn't see the point in having pages for people who weren't even sitting close to the popular table at lunch.

"I hope so too," I responded, since it would be rude to reassure her that it probably would stay that way. "I'm sure if the principal finds out, the site will just be taken down anyway."

"But how?" Tierra asked. "You can't make someone delete a site unless you know who created it, right?"

I hadn't thought about it that way, and I'd carefully considered what would happen if the principal found out. It just showed how much I still needed to learn. The principal could issue all the commands he wanted, but if SlamBook remained up and nobody knew who'd created the slam book for our school, what could he do?

"Go to the person who runs the whole site," I said, stating the answer to my own question out loud without realizing it.

"Huh?" Tierra asked.

"Somebody had to set the thing up in the first place, right?" I said. "When you go to the main page, they have you pick your school."

"So, there are other schools?" she asked.

"Yep."

"Wow. I thought it was just us."

She looked seriously bothered by this, which made me

curious. "Mean people are everywhere," I commented, hoping she'd speak up about whatever was bugging her.

"I guess so," she said. Her forehead was all wrinkled, and she seemed to be thinking hard about something. "Well, I have to go. My mom's waiting outside." She paused. "Do you need a ride?"

"My mom's coming," I said, even though riding home with Tierra would have been nice. "She's picking Hope up from gymnastics practice in about ten minutes, then coming for me."

Looking at the clock on my computer, I realized just how little time I had left at the library. After dinner I could hop back on and try this some more, but I really wanted to figure this out. I'd be obsessed with it until I did.

"No prob," she said.

She stood, and I saw the spine of the book she'd been holding. All I saw were the words "be" and "happier." It was some kind of self-help book about being happier? Was this connected to her crying outside the school? Did this have something to do with the cheating scandal Amy had mentioned? I wasn't going to ask Tierra, so I'd probably never know.

"See you around, I guess," she said as she stepped away. Then she turned and walked out.

I meant to go directly back to my computer, but I found myself staring at her as she walked out. It was the most we had said to each other in a long time, aside from the really short non-conversation we'd had outside school. I hoped she was okay—she seemed sad about something. Did it have to do with the book she was carrying out?

I couldn't answer that question, so I jumped right to what I could control. And that was trying to figure out how to get information on the people posting on Slam-Book. That meant discovering the password to the admin account.

But something else was distracting me. Tierra had mentioned my page on the site. Someone had posted something? I knew that I should ignore it and work on figuring out how to get into SlamBook, but I had to know. It was like someone had just set a big pizza in front of me and the aroma was wafting over to me, despite the fact that I was trying to ignore it. I had to look.

Gritting my teeth, I clicked on the link to my slam book page in my bookmarks toolbar. There was more than one comment now. Many, many comments more than one. Every person who commented was assigned a number, so there were plenty of skipped numbers. Person number forty-two had written one word about me, and it wasn't a nice word. Number fifty-seven was the next comment after that, saying I was a snob. Below that, person fifty-nine had commented about my frizzy hair and bony body, saying I looked like a broom turned upside down.

My hand immediately went to my hair. I'd tried every conditioner, but nothing had helped, especially when there was any moisture in the air at all. Like in spring. And summer. And when it rained or snowed.

But it bothered me more that people thought I was snobby and mean. I felt like I was nice to everyone, but I didn't exactly have the confidence to just go around talking to people. I pretty much assumed nobody had any idea who I was, outside of being "Janelle and Adria's friend."

One look at my page led me over to Adria's page, where the comments I'd seen earlier that day were still there. I couldn't tell if more comments had been posted since lunchtime, but it was mostly nice comments except for the few horrible ones. I found it interesting that it was so easy to notice the nasty comments, even when there were so many positive ones.

"We're waiting for you."

I'd been so caught up in reading Adria's page, I hadn't even noticed that my sister had snuck up behind me. I nearly jumped off my chair when she spoke. I pushed my laptop screen down so fast, it made a large clapping noise. The last thing I wanted was for my sister to find out about SlamBook.

"What'cha doing?" Hope asked, eyeing my laptop suspiciously.

"Research for my project," I lied. Well, it was sort of a lie. Technically what I was learning would help me be better with computers and stuff. So, it was kind of research.

"Well, Mom's been texting you," she said.

"I had my phone on silent."

Duh. I was in the library. Phones were supposed to be silent in the library. But Hope had a point. I should've been watching my phone for a text to come through. At the very least, I could have been keeping an eye on the time and gone outside when I was supposed to. Tierra had thrown me off.

"Coming," I said, shoving my laptop into my backpack. Then I zipped the bag and hopped up to follow Hope to the car.

If she was suspicious, she was over it. She rushed out to the car, assuming I'd be behind her, I guessed. It wouldn't be a big deal if Hope found out about SlamBook. I just didn't want her getting Mom involved before I figured out what was going on.

Hope jumped into the front seat, leaving me with the back seat. No big deal, but it was interesting that it was always assumed that Hope would get the front seat because she was older. That would never change, I now realized, although soon Hope would drive her own car and maybe I'd get Mom to myself. In the car, anyway.

"How did it go?" Mom asked, looking at me in the rear-view mirror.

If Mom had been impatient that I hadn't answered her texts, it didn't show. But my mom didn't really lose her temper. She had that whole meditation-style Zen thing going on where it seemed like nothing could puncture the bubble of happiness around her.

"Fine," I said. "I saw Tierra."

Now, why had I said that? The last thing I wanted to talk about was the friend who had suddenly disappeared from my life at some point along the way. My family had never really interrogated me about that. I was pretty sure they'd asked once where Tierra had been lately, and when I'd just shrugged and said I didn't know, they'd left it alone.

"What's she up to now?" Mom asked.

"She was checking out a book on how to be happier," I said. "Weird, huh?"

As long as we were talking about it, I might as well get their thoughts on it. Maybe they'd come up with something I hadn't thought of.

"Maybe she's sad she isn't your friend anymore," Hope commented. "I hate losing friends. It sucks."

Hope seemed to have a billion friends. Every chance she could, she slept over at someone's house, especially in the summertime. I rarely did sleepovers. Janelle and Adria just didn't seem to ever have them. One reason I was afraid to invite them over to my house was because I was terrified they'd get all "bestie" on me and shut me out of the conversation.

"I don't think so," I said. "She has friends."

I didn't know their names, but I saw her sitting with a couple of girls at lunch every day. Maybe that was why someone had called me a snob. I didn't get to know everyone in my grade. But did most people get to know everyone? How much time did people have? I was busy trying to keep up with my own friends, as well as all that I needed to know to pass my classes and develop my app.

"I guess you just grew apart, huh?" Mom asked.

"That happens sometimes," Hope said, as though she were some wise woman who had lived a thousand lifetimes or something. I just rolled my eyes.

"Yeah, lots of people make different friends when they move from elementary school to middle school," I said, pulling my phone out of my backpack and unlocking it. I could see all of Mom's missed texts on the main screen, but I didn't read them in detail. I wanted to see the comments about me again. I just stared at them.

Who would say those things? I had to know. I had a feeling that when I did find out, I wouldn't even recognize the names. I doubted that anyone who knew me would say such mean things about me. Besides, I just didn't know that many people.

In the front seat, I could hear Mom and Hope talking about yoga. Hope was going with Mom after school the next day. Real exciting. I couldn't help but notice they never invited me. Not that I wanted to go. But it didn't make me feel all that good that they didn't ask.

It was like I was invisible. Except on SlamBook. My page there reminded me that people knew exactly who I was. Even if they didn't have nice things to say about me, at least I wasn't invisible. Being invisible sucked.

I had to hold myself back from throwing the car door open the second Mom pulled into the garage. Inside I could get online and deal with SlamBook. I could really dig down and try to figure things out once I was on my laptop again. Hopefully I'd get a couple of hours of peace and quiet before dinner.

"Uh-uh," Mom said when she saw me sprinting for the door. "Before you go locking yourself in your room, I need your help."

I stopped and turned, my hand on the door to the

house. Seriously? Help with what? Now was not the time for chores.

"We're backed up on laundry," Mom said. "If you want fresh underwear, I'm going to need you to bring all of your clothes and put them in the washer. After that, there are some socks in the dryer we all need to fold."

Great. What happened to being invisible? I wanted to go back to that.

I knew better than to whine about it, though. The best thing to do when Mom had her mind made up about something was to just do it. Besides, normally I'd be fine with helping out. I just had this unhealthy fixation on a certain gossip website.

I headed straight to my room and stuffed all of my laundry into the big bag it was supposed to be in all the time. It took a few minutes, so when I got to the washer, Hope was already there, dumping her clothes in. I knew I should have a good attitude about it, like she did. Helping Mom out was the right thing to do.

"There's room for yours," Hope said, walking off and leaving me to start the washer and get the socks out of the dryer. I had no idea where Mom had gone, but if they weren't going to help, I'd do it. The sooner the socks were folded, the sooner I could get to my computer.

But Mom came barreling in from somewhere in the house just as I was walking toward the kitchen table, arms loaded with as many socks as I could hold. I was dropping them along the way. Giggling, she swept down behind me to pick up as many as she could, then rushed to follow me into the kitchen.

We dumped all of the socks onto the table, then rushed back to see if we'd missed any. Once we had them all, we played the "match game" that Mom had made this into when we were kids. It had been much more fun a few years ago.

"That one's blue," Hope said suddenly, startling me out of my thoughts. I'd been matching, folding, and tossing socks into the pile without really thinking about it.

"Yeah?" I said, looking at the pair of navy-blue socks my sister was holding up.

"The other one's black," Hope said.

"No, it's not. It's blue."

Hope sighed. "Mom," she whined. "These don't match, do they?"

Mom had been lost in her own thoughts, folding away. But the pair of socks Hope was holding just inches from her face pulled her out of it.

"Nope," Mom said.

Sighing again, Hope separated the socks and started looking for their matches. Apparently she'd appointed herself sock-matching expert and I was just the lowly sister who didn't know the difference between navy blue and black.

I thought of all the things people had said about me and my friends on SlamBook. I mean, it wasn't like being good at sock matching was a personality trait or anything. There were far worse things people could say about me, for sure. I just gritted my teeth and stared down at the pile of socks in front of me.

I thought back to what someone had said about Adria earlier that day. Just pure ignorance. They'd insulted her looks and her race, which was silly, considering she'd been born in America. I had to do something about that. As soon as I finished matching socks, I needed to get back to my laptop and figure out a way to get to the usernames of those posting these slams. I'd then decide what to do about the people who were saying nasty things.

Tell Adria?

Tell everyone?

Blast them on their own SlamBook pages?

"Hope and I can finish this if you have something better to do," Mom said.

It took me a second to realize she was speaking to me. I looked up. They were both staring at me.

"You're not really helping," Hope said. "You're kind of in your own world over there."

Oh. She was right about that. I was supposed to be fully interacting with my mom and sister, not worrying about SlamBook.

"Sorry," I said. "I'm here."

I grabbed a few socks and held them up against each other. Dad's brown sock and a black sock. Those were definitely different. I wouldn't mess those up.

Now that I was paying attention, though, I could hear Hope and Mom chitchatting away like I wasn't even there. Same as in the car. Every day. And everywhere else we ever were as a threesome. It hadn't always been that way, but for the past year or so, I'd always just on the outside with the two of them. It was part of why I spent so much time on my computer when I was at home. It was the only place where I felt like I fit in.

"I think I'll ask for a new yoga mat for my birthday," Hope said. "Maybe a pink one?"

I tossed my most recent pair of socks onto the pile and made an executive decision. I was leaving. If they asked why, I'd just say I had homework. That was true, but I had some important things to do first.

I'm not sure why I had an excuse prepared. I knew better. They didn't even notice when I left. I quietly shut the door to my room and scooted behind my desk. I wondered if they ever even noticed I was gone.

CHAPTER 7

Janelle: We can make pages for people!!!

After dinner, I was staring at my computer screen, frustrated, when Janelle's text came through. I stared down at my phone before looking back at my computer monitor. My own page was pulled up, still only populated with the same comments that had been there earlier that day. Nothing new at all. But I'd been looking at the source code for the page to hopefully pull something from it. Going through it line by line was making my eyes ache. I decided to reply to Janelle to procrastinate a little.

Me: **On SlamBook?**

Of course, I knew she meant SlamBook, but I was trying to get her to give more information without saying anything on my end. Sure enough, a few seconds later, my phone buzzed again.

Janelle: **Click this link.**

Her message contained a link, so it was just easier to pull it up on my phone. Plus, that meant I wouldn't have to lose the page of source code I'd been studying on my laptop. I needed to mark my place so I could continue to move down once I finished looking at whatever Janelle was up to now.

The link took me straight to a page for Tierra Ford. The same Tierra I'd just seen at the library. Janelle surely hadn't set up a page for her.

I pushed the button to launch a video chat with Janelle. We did that sort of thing, usually when we were really deep into gossip about something. In fact, sometimes I got the feeling that Janelle sent a text just to get us fired up so we'd video-call her.

She answered on the first ring. Her face filled the screen. She had her hair up in a messy bun, and her face was covered in some type of green beauty goo. She was all into beautification.

"What exactly are you up to?" I asked.

"I made a page for Tierra," she said. "Just to see if I could. It's super easy. You should make a page for someone too."

I got that. But what I didn't get was why she'd chosen Tierra. I also didn't get why she'd had to write that Tierra was a "total loser" in all caps. That was the only comment Tierra had.

But wait. I could work with this. The fact that it was the only slam meant I could compare the IP address associated with that comment to the IP address of the person who'd created this page. That would help me learn more about how this site was set up. Once I had that information, maybe I could find a way to figure out who was posting what. But I had no idea how to get those IP addresses.

I needed help. But first I needed some information from Janelle.

"Where did you go to create this page?" I asked.

"Huh?" She was looking at something else in the room—probably her TV—and not paying a bit of attention to me. But suddenly she seemed to remember I was there. "The main page. There's a link to add new pages."

"Cool," I said. "But why Tierra?"

She shrugged. "Why not? She was fresh on my mind because I saw her moping around outside school when I left. I mean, what a loser."

I held back the urge to defend Tierra, surprised at how strong that urge actually was. Our friendship might have been over, but I still felt this weird loyalty to her. Maybe it was because I'd seen her crying that day outside school. Or maybe it was just that she'd been so nice to me in the library. Whatever it was, I couldn't let Janelle see it.

"Are you going to add other pages?" I asked.

No way would *I* add more pages to this mess. I was busy trying to figure out how to out the people who were being nasty and racist and horrible. Adding more pages would just give them more room for their terribleness.

"I don't know," Janelle said. "Depends who ticks me off. If I find out who's posting things about me, I'm going to be busy making their lives miserable."

She laughed at her own comment, but I was too distracted to laugh with her. Janelle had no idea that I saw figuring this out as a real possibility. She probably just thought maybe she could match the tone of the comments to actual people. But if I could match who was posting what, what was the plan? How would I make their lives miserable?

"What's your username?" I asked Janelle, grabbing a slip of paper and pen to write down what she said. I didn't know if I'd need the information, but it couldn't hurt to have it on hand.

Janelle handed off the information and hung up, leaving me sitting there, biting my lip and staring at my screen. I had a bad habit of doing that when I was trying to figure something out, and I was totally at a loss now. I couldn't get any further with this without some help. And there was one person I knew who could help me more than anyone else.

My mentor. My coding club coach. Ms. Wang.

I thought through all the things that had kept me from asking her before. I didn't want her to ask questions. I didn't want her finding out about SlamBook and telling other people, like my mom or the principal of our school. But I could get the information I needed without telling her serious details, right? I'd just tell her it was a social media thing.

I sent Ms. Wang an email to ask if she was available to chat. For all I knew, she was tutoring someone else or hanging out with friends or working on her own projects. I didn't even really know what her life was like, just that she was an applications developer as her day job and did coding club on the side.

After staring at my screen for a few minutes, I decided she probably wasn't going to get back to me, and I dove back into staring at the source code for the slam page Janelle had just created for Tierra. But as soon as I took my attention off my mailbox, the notification that I had a video message went off. Ms. Wang wanted a face-to-face chat with me.

I bit back my nervousness. Not able to fully understand why I felt that way, I rushed to open the message before Ms. Wang disappeared. I wasn't even sure what I'd say once I was speaking to her.

"What's going on?" Ms. Wang said. "Stuck?"

I was stuck, but not on my app. All that question did was remind me that I was behind on the work I was supposed to be doing. I had to get past this stuff with Slam-Book so I could focus on other things.

"I'm helping a friend with a problem," I said. "She's being trashed on this website, and she wants to know who's doing the trashing. Can I find out who made the posts? Maybe by IP address?"

"Unless you have some kind of analytics tracking, no," Ms. Wang said. "Depends on the site. If you can get the IP address, you can track it using certain software. I'll send you a link. There's also the option of somehow breaking in and getting the username. I'll send you some links for that as well. Do you want to send me the page and let me take a look at it?"

"That's okay," I said, pushing down the panic that was rising. I would have loved for Ms. Wang to take over and just extract a list of names and the numbers SlamBook's database had assigned them when they created their accounts.

Wait a minute. That was all I needed. The master list of which username went with which number, since each of us was assigned a number. With a little more work, I should be able to figure it out. The password hack was probably what I wanted most.

But I knew it wouldn't be easy. None of this stuff was ever easy. Even experts like Ms. Wang would have a hard time getting into sites. That was the whole purpose of security, after all.

Before I'd even hung up, I was squinting at the numbers on Tierra's page. Then comparing them to the numbers on all the other different pages. I was looking for patterns and studying source code and somehow, along the way, I figured out how to get to the master list. It really wasn't complicated at all. The name of the file with the master list of numbers was in the source code of every single page.

And that was how, without ever having to guess a password or use an IP address, I got the list of every single person who was posting on SlamBook for our school.

CHAPTER 8

I was looking right at the person who'd commented on my frizzy hair and bony body. The girl who'd said I looked like a broom turned upside down. It was that Susannah girl from the yearbook staff, the one who had been so excited that Damen King was being trashed on the site.

"Okay, smile!" she told us in a gushy-fake voice as she held her professional-looking camera in front of her face. I leaned closer to Janelle and gave my biggest smile.

Susannah snapped the picture, then kissed up to Janelle some more. At least I wasn't the only one she was ignoring. She was ignoring Adria, too, which was no surprise since she'd posted the awful comment about Adria.

Yeah, I was holding in some anger about that one. Revenge was a dish best served cold, or so my mom's mom always said. Mom said that meant that if you're angry, you don't come up with the best idea to get back at someone. Instead you needed to calm down, think things through, and take action later, once you were calm, cool, and collected.

"I can't wait to see it," Janelle gushed back.

She'd been overly nice to people lately in the hopes that they'd post nice things about her. It was too late with Susannah, though. She'd already posted that Janelle *thinks she's all that but in reality, she's all* not, whatever that was supposed to mean. Janelle had read that comment to us, making fun of it, but I had a feeling it had hurt her.

I wondered what Janelle would do if she knew the person in front of her right now was the one who'd written it. Would she confront Susannah or try to be even nicer to change Susannah's mind? I had a feeling she'd try to change the girl's mind. Janelle liked for people to like her. It was important to her.

"We need to go," I said to Janelle. "We'll be late for homeroom."

Both Janelle and Susannah looked at me with shocked expressions. Janelle had a frozen smile, and Susannah's smile had disappeared altogether. They couldn't believe I was interrupting their conversation. Whatever. Unlike Janelle, I wasn't going to be nice to people just so they'd like me. Especially people who were writing mean things about us online.

"What's going on with you?" Adria asked once we were speeding toward class. "That was kind of rude."

"I just don't want to be late," I said.

This was the part about decoding SlamBook that would be the hardest. I couldn't tell my friends what I'd found out, but I wasn't very good at bottling up my emotions. I hadn't quite thought about what it would be like to face the very people who were slamming us.

Like Amy. Mean, mean, mean Amy Tatem.

There she was in homeroom, smiling at Janelle like she was Janelle's long-lost best friend. Only, she was the same person who had made some snarky comment about Janelle's red hair. Not to mention the many nasty things she'd written about pretty much every girl who had a page on there other than Tierra. I was sure she'd get to Tierra soon enough. She couldn't seem to pass up the opportunity to pick the one physical flaw people had and blow it up into a huge deal.

Who would have thought?

"Did you hear?" she asked before we'd even sat down.

Uh-oh. Who would she be talking about now?

"Tierra was slammed," she said. "Seriously slammed. Look at her page."

She was talking to Janelle, but her words caused a knot to form in the pit of my stomach. That was exactly what I'd been afraid would happen. Tierra's page had turned nasty. I wondered if Amy was one of the people posting mean things. I could certainly find out. Amy was number fourteen.

Since the two of them were chitchatting away, I pulled up Tierra's SlamBook page on my phone. I didn't have long, but it wouldn't take long. Just the SlamBook URL and Tierra's first and last name.

Sure enough, there were a few comments that had popped up since I'd last looked. Most were fairly harmless.

Slams like "lame" and "boring" were no surprise. Pretty much all of us had that at least once by now. But the one calling her a cheater was a bit of a surprise. It shouldn't have been, since that was the going rumor about her, but I knew it hurt. I wondered if that was what Amy was talking about.

I scrolled down to number fourteen and had my answer. Just two words. But they were two words that packed a big punch.

"Mentally unbalanced."

Wow. All the comments were bad. But like Adria's comment, this one was one of the worst. I wondered how long it would be before people connected the number fourteen with the worst of all possible comments.

I'd never seen anything about Tierra that would make someone say that about her except, maybe, that she'd been crying outside of school that day. But that just made her a human being with feelings. We all cried when we got upset, and if Tierra really had been accused of cheating, crying was the response most of us would have.

But then I thought about it. Tierra couldn't win with this comment. If she got upset about it, people would just say that proved person number fourteen was right. The comment was actually clever, in a horrible, devious sort of way.

As homeroom started, I occasionally looked at Amy out of the corner of my eye. She was a real piece of work. There she sat, staring at the teacher as though she were Little Miss Innocent, all the while being a backstabber behind the scenes. It made me want to go straight to her page and post something nasty. Something that would cut her to the core. Then I'd just come right back into homeroom and act like I knew nothing about such a thing being posted.

And while I was at it, I wanted to go after Susannah, then anyone else who had posted nasty things behind someone's back, only to smile to that person's face. But that would require far more than cracking the site's code. That would mean some serious creativity.

I had a little time at the start of first period, so I spent it on my phone while everyone around me was happily chit-chatting. Amy was one of the few people who still didn't have a page. That was just weird to me, considering how active she was. But I could fix that. I'd just set one up for her. The only problem was, the person running the page would be able to see that I'd done that. What if Amy was the one who'd created our school's slam book?

Nah. She would've made sure she had a page first if she'd done that. In fact, I was surprised she hadn't created one for herself anyway. Unless . . .

Unless she was afraid what people might post about her.

I could take care of that. Right there, in class, I created a page for Amy. I clicked the button to add a comment and paused while I thought through my strategy. I could post some bad stuff right away, but maybe I should wait to see how long this page could remain blank. That would send a message to Amy that nobody had anything to say about her. Once the first comment had been posted, then I'd double back and post something. That would give me time to come up with the perfect insult.

And now for Susannah . . .

Unlike Amy, Susannah had a page. I went back to the list of names and clicked on hers. There were plenty of nice comments, along with a couple of nasty blows referencing how she thought she was all that because she was on the honor roll. Those wouldn't really cut to the core, though. I closed my eyes and pictured the Susannah I'd seen that morning. The one who had been nice to Janelle to her face while posting horrible things behind her back.

This one was easy.

Smiles to your face while stabbing you in the back, I typed into the POST YOUR SLAM box.

Perfect because it was true. Perfect because it would harm Susannah more than insulting her directly. How many friends would shy away from her based on what I posted? How many people would wonder if the slams they read on the website were from her?

I smiled my way through first period, then second. But on the way to third, I started having doubts. This wasn't really the person I wanted to be, was it? I wanted to make things better, not worse.

It didn't help that Susannah was in my third-period class. She always sat at the front, raising her hand to answer every single teacher question. Yes, she was *that* person. Her BFF Ani sat across the aisle from her, and they always talked only to each other, no one else.

I took my seat at the back of the class and watched the two of them. Ani hadn't checked SlamBook since first period, probably. Maybe she didn't know about it at all.

When she saw what I posted, though, maybe she'd think twice about her good friend, especially if she wondered whether Susannah had gossiped about her.

The more I watched the two of them, the angrier I got. Susannah had posted so many nasty things and gotten away with it. I had a feeling Ani wouldn't care unless she suspected Susannah was slamming *her*.

And that could be arranged. . . .

Class had started, so I couldn't get on my phone. The last thing I needed was to have it confiscated and turned in to the principal. I had work to do between classes.

On my way to lunch, I managed to set up a page for Ani and check that nobody else had left other comments for Susannah. I wondered if people even knew they had pages. They weren't super popular or anything. I bottled up my excitement and walked into the cafeteria, hopping into line behind a group of giggly seventh graders.

"Where have you been?"

I jumped at the sound of Janelle's voice. She had snuck up behind me and put her face close to my ear for effect. I turned around and saw that she was alone. Usually she and Adria traveled as a pair.

"Class," I said.

"Between classes," Janelle said. "I haven't seen you since homeroom."

She was right. I usually made a point to track Janelle down, but not today. Today I'd rushed to each class, plopped down in my seat, and gone straight to my phone. This SlamBook thing was really infecting my brain.

"It's all blowing up in the comments," she said. "I was trying to track you down to tell you."

I immediately assumed she was talking about Slam-Book, but then I wondered if I just had SlamBook on the brain.

"What?" I asked.

"SlamBook, of course," she said. "Did you know there's a comments section on the main page?"

I'd noticed that at some point, but mostly it had been a bunch of junk. Shout-outs and greetings and nonsense. I'd forgotten about it after that.

"What do you mean, it's blowing up?" I asked.

"People are freaking out," she said, emphasizing those last two words. "And everyone's anonymous, so there's a bunch of trolling. It's just a mess."

We'd reached the trays by then, and I grabbed one, as well as a fork. I wasn't really all that hungry all of a sudden. Mostly I wanted to just hop onto my phone and enjoy all the drama. But I knew that wasn't good for me. I had to stop letting SlamBook suck me in.

Janelle grabbed a tray and fork too and followed me through the line. She never joined me there. She always brought her lunch and stayed with Adria. This was kind of . . . nice.

But then we got to the lunch lady. I ordered the enchiladas and some rice. Janelle ordered the same. Now she was copying my lunch choices.

Okay, what was going on?

"Yum!" Adria said when Janelle plopped her tray down next to her. Adria was eating her usual sandwich. Despite the fact that Janelle and I were eating the exact same thing, Adria's comment was directed only at Janelle.

"Did you tell her?" Adria asked Janelle around a mouthful of sandwich.

"Yeah. She hasn't seen it yet."

"The comments section?" I asked. "She told me. So people are pretty upset?"

"The backlash is here," Adria said. "Only, instead of going to the principal or parents or whatever, they're starting all these threads about 'Why are you people so mean?' Bunch of whiners."

"At least they're trying to make a difference," I said. "Is that so bad?"

I looked at Janelle because I knew she was on my side in this. Right? She wanted SlamBook taken down. She thought it was wrong.

Janelle shoved a forkful of rice into her mouth. That meant we had to wait until she finished chewing and swallowed before we could hear her answer.

Finally she shrugged. "Life sucks. People say mean things about each other. If you don't like it, don't read it."

I wanted to start eating my own lunch before it got cold, but suddenly I couldn't move. I was frozen, just staring at her.

"I thought you wanted SlamBook taken down," I finally managed to say.

She looked over at Adria, then back at me. Something about the expression on her face told me I was way behind. How was that my fault, though? They could have texted me at any time and updated me on the fact that they were now pro-SlamBook.

"That was before there were so many pages," Adria said. "The focus is off Janelle. Now it's, like, *everyone's* problem."

"And the things they wrote about you?" I asked Adria.

Her expression darkened slightly. "Yeah, that's not right."

"But slamming other people is the best revenge," Janelle said. "I mean, it's not like you can't figure out who wrote those things. We all know who the horrible people are in our school."

Did we, really? Because last time I'd checked, Janelle was having a great laugh with the very girl who had attacked her the worst.

"So you've slammed those people?" I asked.

Obviously I was way behind. I hadn't followed Janelle's and Adria's comments. Once I'd discovered what Susannah and Amy had written, I'd spent so much time looking at their comments everywhere that I hadn't gotten around to anyone else. And the more pages that were created, the harder it would become.

"The point is, people are free to say whatever they want in the comments," Janelle said. "It's not going to change anything. Maybe I'll post my own comment."

"Me too," Adria said. "I'll point out how unoriginal these people are that all they can think to do is slam people's looks. Go for something deeper."

I munched happily on my enchilada while looking from Adria to Janelle. Hmm . . . Maybe there was something here. I should have been watching the comments section on the main page too. I wondered if there was a way to get back at the people making nasty slams by posting what I knew in the main comments area.

I stuck a bookmark into that thought and took another bite of enchilada. But I'd barely gotten a bite in when Amy slid onto the seat next to me.

Great. Just great. Not what I needed right then.

"Did you see it?" she asked no one in particular. At least, no one that I could tell. She was probably talking to Janelle, though. She always spoke primarily to Janelle.

"What?" Janelle asked, her expression all innocence.

Shaking my head to myself, I focused on my lunch. I

didn't want to go through this conversation again, especially not with the girl who had just anonymously called Tierra "mentally unbalanced."

"The comments," she said. "It's a battle zone in there."

"Whatever," Janelle said as if she hadn't just been gossiping about it. "No big deal."

Adria didn't seem to know what to say to that. Neither did I. The convo would just stall if none of us cared what Amy had to say.

"What are they saying?" I asked.

Yeah, I'd be the bad guy. What I really wanted to know was if Amy had seen her page yet. Or if she'd noticed that nobody had left any comments. At the very least, maybe she'd inspire me to come up with a really good slam against her. Something that would cut deep.

"Just a bunch of stuff about how everyone sucks," Amy said. "That pretty much sums it up. But someone said they know how to get in and delete the whole thing, and everyone's challenging that. I mean, nobody would know how to do anything like that, would they?"

Silence. I looked at Janelle and Adria, who seemed to be thinking through that possibility. I decided this was the perfect opportunity to plant a little seed that might come in handy later.

"Do you know how many people are in this school?" I asked, gesturing to indicate the cafeteria full of people. "There have to be at least a few coders here. Some app developers, maybe a few of those people who hack into stuff just to see if they can. What do they call those people?"

Friendly hackers, that was what they were called. But I had to pretend I didn't know that.

"Criminals?" Adria asked.

"No, she's talking about the dudes who help police officers and stuff," Amy said.

"It's not just dudes," I blurted before I could stop myself. Even worse, I sounded annoyed. I took a deep breath and tried to sound less personally interested. "I saw a show on it once on that crime channel. These people hack into sites to show how not safe they are."

"Cool," Janelle said. "So someone could just hack into SlamBook and figure out who was posting what?"

Now they were getting a little too close to the truth. I didn't like that. I needed to change the subject, quickly.

"Or you could read the comments," I said. "I don't

know. Maybe you could guess someone's personality by the way they write things."

That was a silly suggestion. It wasn't like people were writing essays about each person. Slams were just a few words—sometimes only one or two. Plus, I would have never guessed that Amy and Susannah were the ones posting the nastiest comments. But the goal was to change the subject.

"I'm going to try that," Adria said. "Maybe I can figure out who was posting about me."

I glanced at Amy out of the corner of my eye—something I hadn't been doing when we'd been discussing hacking. Was she nervous that we might figure out she was the one doing the mean posting? I couldn't tell. She wasn't smiling anymore, but her expression was pretty neutral.

"Well, I have to get back to my table," Amy said. "Let me know what you figure out. See you around."

Was it my imagination, or had her exit been extremely sudden? It was as if she'd gotten nervous about the conversation and rushed off. Were we hitting a little too close to home?

That thought made me angrier than I'd expected. Amy

had a lot of nerve. Just thinking she could post horrible things about everyone and bounce around, being nice to our faces. How many other people were doing that too? The whole back-stabbiness of SlamBook was infuriating.

I had to do something. I had to get in there and show the Amys and Susannahs of the school how it felt to log in and see horrible things about you. I had to make sure the comments I posted really hurt.

And then we'd all be even. Then things would be better. They had to be.

CHAPTER 9

Friday nights were for pizza. Veggie gluten-free for Hope, and pepperoni and sausage for the rest of us. Hope had decided a year before that she was going to be *super* healthy. I always enjoyed the pepperoni on my slices a little more when Hope glanced my way. Not that she envied me or anything, but it made me feel a little better.

"What's going on in your world, Faith?" Dad asked. He'd been working so much, we hadn't had time to catch up lately. The problem was, I couldn't really tell the full truth. So I told the part of the truth I could.

"Just working on my project," I said with a shrug.

"How's it going?" he asked.

"Sort of good," I said. "I'm stuck on this one thing."

When I wasn't going after everyone who had written something mean on SlamBook, I'd spent every waking non-school hour plugging away at my app. I'd barely gotten enough done to justify even having a meeting with Ms. Wang. I had to catch up.

"Can Google help?" Dad asked.

"It's . . . complicated," I said with a frown.

I glanced at Hope and Mom. They both were focused on their pizza. In other words, bored senseless by this convo. Which meant I needed to change the subject ASAP.

"Janelle's mom got a new car," I blurted.

Of course, nobody cared about Janelle's mom's new car, even if it was a sports car and supercool. But my mom at least stopped staring at her pizza.

"What kind?" she asked.

"Red."

"Make? Model?"

That came from Dad. Oh right. I'd forgotten he was way into cars and stuff. I just shrugged.

"It's a sports car," I said.

"Can I spend the night at Amber's house tomorrow night?" Hope suddenly blurted out.

Annnnd . . . I'd lost them. Just like that. The conversation switched away from me and right onto Hope, who would spend the next five minutes answering questions about whether Amber's parents would be home and if they'd be leaving the house during this proposed sleepover.

"May I be excused?" I asked.

Nobody answered. They were mid-interrogation. I couldn't expect more. I had too much to do to sit there and watch an argument like it was a bad reality show.

I quietly shut my bedroom door, just in case someone cared that I'd left, and plopped down onto the bed with my laptop. I'd been in a great pattern lately of forcing myself to do an hour of coding work before I could even think about checking SlamBook. But it was Friday night and I'd finished my work. I deserved this little break.

I started with my own page. Nothing new. My page had stalled at the initial comments people had left for me. Once there were other pages, people had lost interest in slamming me. No surprise. I was just glad people had known who I was.

I scrolled through Adria's page. The nasty comments burned me up, but they'd been left far behind. Suddenly I didn't see those, noticing only the comments that she was sweet, so beautiful, a great friend to Janelle.

Yes, someone had posted that. *A great friend to Janelle.* Like that was an actual personality quality. It annoyed me in a way, I hated to admit. Even though I was still upset that Adria had received some harsher comments, I couldn't help but think about all the times Adria had pushed me out of conversations and told me what to do. Now, without allowing time for me to talk myself out of it, I clicked the button to post a comment and wrote the one thing that made me feel better.

A Janelle Tenning wannabe.

I pressed post, and then sat back and smiled. That would do it. That would make her maybe reconsider how she kissed up to Janelle all the time. It was ridiculous. Get your *own* personality, girl! She'd look at this and think about maybe becoming her own person, I was sure of it.

Pushed forward by that surge of adrenaline, I pulled up Amy's page. Her words about Tierra were still stuck in my mind, in bold print. "Mentally unbalanced."

I was ready. Ready to get back at Amy. I took a deep breath and typed the comment I'd been rolling around in my brain all day.

Loudmouthed know-it-all try-hard.

It was low. Way low. And wrong. But it fit Amy totally. Others had gone after her looks, her weight, her crooked teeth. None of that was wrong with Amy at all. It was just silly. But "try-hard" fit her exactly. In our school, being called a try-hard was even worse than being a loser. It meant no matter how hard you tried—to be popular, cool, likable, whatever—you failed. Over and over and over again. Which just made you desperate.

I sat back and admired my handiwork. I tried to picture the look on Amy's face when she saw it. I wished I could be there, but I knew there was no way that would happen. Maybe she'd mention it in homeroom on Monday. I could hope.

My phone buzzed next to me. Video chat request from Janelle. I quickly slammed my laptop shut, like she could see what I was doing or something, and answered the phone.

"I'm bored," Janelle whined without even saying hello. "What'cha got going on over there?"

If she'd called me for excitement, she'd be super disappointed. Nothing exciting where I was. Checking SlamBook was pretty much the highlight of my whole day. Pathetic. Just pathetic.

"Just finished dinner," I said. Not a lie.

"What did you have?"

"Pizza."

"Cool," Janelle said. Although there was nothing really all that cool about hanging out at my house on a Friday night. But Janelle was just sitting around at home too.

"Now I'm just figuring out what to do," I said. "Maybe watch something on my laptop."

She'd think I meant TV, but "watch something on my laptop" could mean a lot of things. Like watching the comments section of SlamBook. Or watching myself put in at least an hour or two of work on my project. But I didn't want to talk about either of those things to Janelle.

"Did you check out the comments on the main page yet?" Janelle asked.

I opened my laptop back up and clicked on the link to go back to the main page for our school. I'd scrolled through the comments page, but most of it was just people fighting about whether or not SlamBook should be taken down. I wasn't interested in reading all that.

"Not recently," I admitted. "Is there something new?"

"Someone claims to have told Mr. Marquez about SlamBook," she said. "He said he'd keep an eye on it."

Oh. I stared at my screen, a slightly sick feeling in the pit of my stomach. What if Mr. Marquez really was watching? What if he found a way to get in and see who was posting what? My name wasn't on my account anywhere, but I knew better than anyone else that if someone really wanted that information, it was gettable.

If they found out who'd posted what, I'd be in big, big trouble. Plenty of people would, but I had to keep in mind that I wasn't innocent.

"Do you think he really is?" I asked Janelle, still staring at my laptop instead of her face on my phone screen. "I mean, do you think he's watching?"

"Maybe," Janelle said. "So what if he does? It's not like he can see who's posting what."

"How do you know that?" I asked. "What if there's a way for him to get in and see everything?"

"I guess people will get in trouble, then," Janelle said.

"We haven't been posting mean things, so we have nothing to worry about."

I looked at Janelle to make sure she was serious. She really was. She'd just been reading the comments on others and not posting anything?

"I guess if tons of people are posting bad things, he can't suspend that many people, right?" I asked. The thought of being suspended from school for posting mean things online terrified me. My parents would be super disappointed, even if I'd been doing it out of revenge.

"Probably could," Janelle said. "I mean, it's bullying, right?"

That word hit me hard. Bullying. I knew this. How many times had we been subjected to lectures on cyberbullying? Yet that was exactly what SlamBook was. Did that make me a cyberbully?

No. I was bullying the bullies. It was okay.

Maybe if I told myself that enough, I'd believe it.

I scrolled down to the comments link for our school's slam book and clicked on it. Sure enough, the very first post said it like it was.

THIS IS BULLYING!!!

 140

There were more than a hundred comments on that one. Posts below it mostly covered the same "This site should be taken down" type of tone, and all had a ton of comments. There were a few "How do I use this site?" types of posts that had very few comments. People seemed to most want to weigh in on the rightness versus wrongness of SlamBook.

I clicked on the "bullying" post and winced. Someone had posted a long rant about the nature of the slams and that many of them went after girls' appearances. Boy slams were more about their smarts and abilities—or lack thereof.

I thought about that for a second. I was proud of myself for at least not going after anyone's appearance. I cut deeper than that. I attacked on a social level. But did that make me any better than the others?

"Hello?" Janelle was saying. "I'm over here."

I realized then that I'd been staring at my screen for a really, really long time. So long that I'd forgotten I was in the middle of a video call with Janelle. SlamBook had that effect on me. I'd lose all concept of time and place.

"Do you think she's right?" I asked.

"Who?" Janelle asked, sipping something through a bright pink reusable straw.

"The girl who said we go after a girl's appearance but a boy's smarts and abilities."

"How do you know it's a girl?"

I looked back at the screen. Good point. There was nothing saying this was written by a girl. Why had I assumed that?

"Most of the slams about me had nothing to do with my looks," Janelle said. "Just what I think about my looks."

I nodded. She was right. Things weren't as bright and shiny on Janelle's page as they'd been the first day we saw her page. Lots of comments about how stuck-up she was and how she *thinks she's all that*. Nothing looks-based where she was concerned. Still, though, it made me uncomfortable how many people had attacked girls based on looks. Especially Adria. She seemed to have gotten it more than anyone else. I wouldn't have been surprised if she was the one who'd posted this ranting comment.

"You just can't take it seriously, that's all," Janelle said. "Anyway, I'm sure it'll be taken down soon. It's only a matter of time, especially now that Mr. Marquez knows about it. He'll bring all this to an end, pronto, bet you."

Before I could answer, there was a knock on my bedroom door. I slapped my laptop shut without even thinking about it. It was like, just by opening that door, whoever was on the other side of it would immediately see what I'd been doing.

"Come in!" I called, keeping Janelle on the phone. People tended to go away when they saw you were chatting with a friend.

"Hey," Hope said, peeking her head in. "Are you busy?"

I looked at my phone. Picked it up to show that Janelle was on the screen.

"Hi!" Janelle called out.

"Hi," Hope said, walking into the room.

"How's cheerleading going? Ready for competition?"

And there they went. Janelle and Hope. Every time the two of them saw each other, they acted like they were the only two people who had ever been cheerleaders. It was their bond. It was a bond I shared with neither of them.

Hope came over and plopped onto my bed, taking my phone. Rolling my eyes, I opened my laptop and pulled up my project. Might as well get some work done.

"Can I talk to my sis for a minute?" Hope asked Janelle before I could even get started.

"Sure!" Janelle said. "Bye-eeee!"

The disgusting thing about that? Hope joined in on that extra-long "bye." I resisted the urge to roll my eyes. Janelle was my friend. I shouldn't think anything she did was cheesy, but when my sister did it, it was *so* cheesy.

"You left," Hope said once I'd hung up with Janelle and set my phone aside.

"Huh?" I asked.

"Dinner," Hope said. "You just got up and left."

"You guys seemed like you were having your conversation," I said with a shrug. "I have work to do."

I turned my laptop around to show her the screen full of code I'd been staring at for the past thirty seconds or so. She barely glanced at it. It could have been SlamBook, and she wouldn't have known the difference, I was pretty sure.

"Something's up with you," Hope said.

Okay, so that got my attention. I closed my laptop and set it aside.

"What do you mean?" I asked, but I had a weird, fluttery feeling in my stomach.

"You've just been . . . different lately. Not talking much, staying to yourself. It's not like you."

Really? I'd always thought of myself as a very quiet person. I would have said I always stayed to myself. But Hope wouldn't have said something if it hadn't been super noticeable.

"Just really stressed out about school stuff," I said. "And my project. It's like there aren't enough hours in the day, you know?"

Hope wasn't buying it. She could always read me.

"Friend stuff sucks," Hope said, even though I'd said nothing at all about friends. "It can totally distract you from what's important."

"And what's that?" I asked. I was just curious where she was going with all this. She'd just come into my room to give me advice?

"Well, friends are important," she said. "But the drama isn't. It sucks you in and holds you there. Just remember that. And no matter what happens, your family has your back. Especially me."

I smiled at her. It seemed like somehow she actually knew what I was dealing with. Drama. Plenty of drama.

More drama than I really could handle. And the more time I spent obsessing over SlamBook, the less time I had for things that were really important, like enjoying a meal with my family and diving into my project—the things that had once made me so happy and now seemed like they were just keeping me away from SlamBook.

Yeah, that. I couldn't do that anymore. Hope was right. I had to stay away from SlamBook.

"You know what?" I asked. "I don't want to work tonight. Let's get Mom and Dad to watch a movie with us."

"Now, that sounds like a plan," Hope said, hopping up. Together, we went to the family room to pick out a movie.

CHAPTER 10

Saturday morning was a win. I stuck to my commitment all morning, enjoying breakfast with the fam and traveling along with my mom and sis as they went to the bookstore. Hope wanted some fashion magazine, and Mom wanted coffee.

Saturday afternoon . . . not so much. Hope was hanging out in her room, watching reality TV and flipping through her magazine. Mom had rushed off to a hair appointment. I busied myself at my laptop, trying to avoid the temptation to look at SlamBook while focusing on my app.

Midway through the afternoon, the texts started coming through.

They were from Janelle. Which would have been a good thing any other day of my life, pretty much. But what she was texting about meant she was the last person I wanted to deal with right then.

Janelle: **Have U checked the comments on the main page?**

Me: **No.**

Janelle: **Go do it. I'll wait.**

I sighed. How should I deal with this? She didn't know I had issues with SlamBook. I could just pretend I was looking at the site, but I had a feeling she was about to ask some questions.

Me: **I can't. 2 depressing.**

There. That should do it. Janelle may have changed her mind, but she couldn't forget that she'd initially hated the whole SlamBook thing. She'd made it her life's mission to get it taken down. She should understand my need to just stay away. Maybe all this secrecy about the comments I'd been leaving was finally paying off. I could stop checking SlamBook altogether without anyone bugging me about it.

Janelle: **Srsly. Go 2 the comments.**

As I sat there, staring at the screen and contemplating just ignoring Janelle for the rest of the day, another text came through. Against my better judgment, I looked at it.

Janelle: **Ppl R freaking.**

Janelle: **This may be what takes the site down. For realz.**

Okay, now she had my attention. What would have people freaking out *that much*? Had someone posted something even meaner than ever before? Was that possible?

With an unhappy grunt, I opened my browser window and typed in the address for SlamBook. My own page on the site had been a shortcut on my desktop from the time I discovered it, but I'd deleted that shortcut the night before to avoid the temptation to go look at the site. So much for that. But I told myself I'd only peek at the comments. Then I'd go back to working on my project.

My heart was racing as I scrolled down the page to the familiar list of hyperlinked words. I told myself it was silly to be nervous about this. I wasn't jumping back into Slam-Book. I was just looking at comments. But my fingers were trembly, there was no denying it.

149

I expected the usual subjects, like *You people suck* and *This site needs to be taken down NOW!* And those were there, for sure. But I knew immediately that the first subject line was the one that had "people freaking," as Janelle had put it.

Can't take this anymore, it read.

There was something so solemn about those words, which looked quiet and dignified at the top of the list of subject lines that were in all caps and written in texting shorthand. There was nothing especially disturbing about the words themselves. I, too, felt like I couldn't take this website anymore, and I was a large part of the problem. But when that subject line was combined with Janelle's text, I knew I had to click to read that subject line's comment.

The message was written by someone going by the username "Sick&Tired." In the main comments section of SlamBook, people could make up usernames rather than going by numbers like we did everywhere else on the site. And yes, I was assuming it was a female since most of the guys at school couldn't care less about SlamBook. Of course, this person could have not even had a page here at all. She might just be sick of seeing everyone else hate on each other.

But then I read her comment, and I knew that wasn't the case.

I've spent the past couple of days checking my page to see what you all have written about me. I can't understand how anyone can be so mean. You sit in the same classes as me. You cheer along with me at basketball and football games. We share the same school pride. Doesn't that matter to any of you?

You insulted my looks. I spent hours staring in the mirror, trying to figure out what I should change. You attacked my personality. I stopped being myself and started walking around paranoid, not knowing which of you I might be offending. I've changed everything for you . . . and it's not enough.

I guess none of you will be happy until I'm gone forever. Fine. I'll give you what you want. But you all need to take a long, hard look at yourselves and realize that you are the ones who need to change. You're horrible, insecure people who make yourselves feel better by putting other people down. I'm ashamed to go to school with all of you.

I didn't realize I'd been holding my breath until I got

to the end of the post. Then I let all that breath out and scrolled down. There were eighty-three replies. The whole school seemed to have come together to tell this girl to please seek help.

There were other comments too. Many were agreeing that SlamBook was rotting our school from the inside out and the principal needed to do something about it. People were saying they were going to the school board and principal and various teachers to report this. Other people were saying that wouldn't help this poor soul, who was obviously at the end of her rope.

But most had the same response I'd had to reading that. We wanted to help. Now. We wanted to undo everything that had been written that had made this girl feel this way. The only problem? We had no idea who this person was. There were now more than two hundred pages on our school's slam book site. We didn't even know if this girl was a sixth grader, seventh grader, or eighth grader. She could be anyone.

She could be someone *I* had insulted. I hadn't gone after anyone's looks, but plenty of other people had. And if we wanted to talk about people who had trashed people's personalities, I was Guilty Person Number One. After what I'd written, I could imagine that quite a few people were walking around wondering who they might have offended by merely speaking.

But even if I hadn't insulted people's looks, I'd hit below the belt. Sure, I could couch it as "getting revenge," but in reality, it was no better than people who threw words around like "skinny fat" and "cankles" when insulting people. In fact, I'd known full well that the insults I was posting would hurt more than some superficial insult would. That made me just as guilty as everyone else.

It all seemed like a bad dream now. Me, sitting in front of this very laptop, adding horrible things to people's pages. Me, walking around school, feeling that thrill of knowing I was hurting people.

I should have been ashamed. I should have realized the damage SlamBook was doing. I should have known that my horrible comments could possibly lead someone to want to disappear.

I picked up my phone and read Janelle's newest text. I hadn't even heard the phone buzz, I'd been so caught up in what I was reading.

Janelle: **U there?**

I only took a couple of seconds to think before I typed a response.

Me: **Who wrote that?**

I hadn't read through all the responses to Sick&Tired's post. For all I knew, someone had identified the student and they were already trying to help her.

Janelle: **No idea.**

I started clicking on comments, trying to get an answer. I couldn't find one where the girl had posted again. Just a bunch of replies where people were asking what we should do and begging her to let us know she was okay. People had taken the *I guess none of you will be happy until I'm gone forever. Fine. I'll give you what you want* part of the post very seriously. Unless she planned to run away, something very, very bad could happen. Even if she ran away, something bad could still happen. It was a dangerous world out there.

And if something happened to Sick&Tired, it could be my fault.

Me: **We have to do something.**

Janelle: **Nothing that we can do.**

 154

Janelle was a good person. Even though she could seem surfacey at times, she had a seriously warm heart. That's one of the reasons I admired her so much. I knew that if she really felt that someone was in trouble, she'd want to help them. She probably didn't take this stuff seriously.

Me: **Do U understand this person plans 2 disappear?**

Silence. Several minutes ticked by, and I had no idea what that meant. Maybe she was rereading the comments and trying to figure out what to make of them. Maybe it was all sinking in. Maybe she was thinking through exactly what we could do to fix this.

Janelle: **She's just saying that.**

Just as I'd thought. Janelle was one of the ones who didn't think there was a danger to SlamBook. It was probably easier to take that route. But if we all dismissed this comment from Sick&Tired, what if something bad happened? What if "gone forever" meant something horrible?

I decided to do what I could to get Janelle to imagine the worst and hope for the best.

Me: **I don't think so.**

While I waited for the next text, my phone rang. It was Janelle.

"What should we do?" she asked.

"I don't know," I said. "Should we call the police?"

Janelle gasped. I knew what she was thinking. If we called the police, the whole school would be in trouble. I could see the website on the evening news, with reporters making a huge deal out of the fact that we were just having a little fun. We'd had no idea it could really hurt someone.

Worst of all, that probably wouldn't do any good, anyway. If the upset student's page ended up plastered all over the evening news, wouldn't that just make things worse?

No, we had to find a better way.

I stared down at my laptop. I had figured out which person went with which assigned line number. Wasn't there a way I could somehow find the names of people posting comments on the main section? There had to be a way to find out who was behind each comment.

Now that the idea had taken hold, I couldn't wait to get started. I mumbled, "Call you back" to Janelle and hung up. She'd probably wonder why I'd hung up when we needed to help this Sick&Tired person, but I didn't have time to think about that.

Just as I was pulling up SlamBook to start working, I heard the scrape of my bedroom door on the doorjamb. Panicked, I spun around in my seat, only realizing once I was facing the door that I hadn't shut my laptop. With Hope staring me down, I didn't have time.

"What's up?" she asked, coming across and sitting down on the edge of my bed.

Still looking at her, I reached up and pulled the laptop closed. I was quick. She couldn't possibly have seen what was on my screen.

"What was that?" she asked.

Oh crud.

"What?" I asked, playing dumb. Then I quickly added, "Just working on a new app."

"It looked . . . interesting," she said, leaning to the left to see my laptop. Even though it was closed. I knew she was dying to crawl over and open that laptop to take a look. She knew better, though. That would be *way* across the line.

"I thought you were watching TV," I commented, hoping to push her past whatever she was thinking.

"I'm bored," she complained. "I think we should do something."

157 ♥

Do something? No way could I do something. But how did I get out of this?

"I have a project due on Monday," I said. "I'm going to be working the rest of the day on it. Like, every second of the rest of the day."

There. That would do it.

"That's so icky," she said. "We could go get frozen custard."

She knew frozen custard was my weakness. Mom probably would go for it too, once she got back from her hair appointment. Which would be any second. But a life could depend on me doing this work.

"You guys go ahead without me," I said. "Maybe bring back a pint for the freezer."

"No," she said. "You're coming. You're always working. A few minutes of fun isn't going to hurt you. Come on."

I didn't budge, even though she stood and walked to the door. I could just turn around and open my laptop again, but what if she came to look over my shoulder? I couldn't risk that.

Before I could try telling her to give me a few minutes, at which point I'd be annoying and ignore her repeated calls for me to "Come on already," the doorbell rang. I breathed a sigh of relief. At the very least, that would maybe give Hope something to do for a little while. It was probably the postal guy with a package, or someone selling internet service.

"Ooh," she said, rushing off.

"Look through the peephole," I yelled after her. That was what Mom was always telling us. It was partly a way to make myself feel more comfortable as I turned around and opened my laptop again.

Then I did something supersmart. I pulled up my project so that when Hope returned, I could quickly flip to that screen. I'd just tell her the other screen she'd seen was my preview page for the app I was developing.

All of a sudden, someone appeared in my doorway. I assumed it was Hope, but when I looked up, I saw Janelle standing there.

"You just hung up," she commented. "I didn't know what to do."

"So you came over?" I asked, stunned. She lived several miles away.

"Mom had to run to the store anyway," she said. "I hitched a ride with her."

I didn't want to say it, but I was actually relieved. I had no idea what I was doing, but I'd feel better if I didn't have to sit there and figure it out alone. The problem was, I couldn't get Janelle's help with something she didn't know I was doing. Well, I could, but it would give away at least one of my secrets.

I scanned the page of comments and clicked on Sick&Tired's post. I stared at the screen. I wasn't looking at it the way others would. No, I was trying to find something in the text that would give away the person's identity.

"Could you do me a favor?" I asked. "Lock that door so my sister doesn't come in."

Janelle nodded. She closed and locked the door, then came over to sit on my bed next to me. We both sat, propped up by pillows, staring at my screen while I tried to figure out what to do.

I went to the page that I knew was a standard log-in for this type of website and started trying basic administrator passwords. None of them worked. I stopped for a second and thought about it. These were my own classmates, not some typical administrator. But if I kept trying to guess, one thing was certain. I'd lock myself out.

"Let's think about this a second," Janelle said. "Has anyone seemed more upset than usual lately?"

My mind immediately went to Tierra. Okay, so my mind had pretty much been on her for the past half hour or so. It was this nagging feeling deep in the back of my brain somewhere that I didn't really want to focus on. Tierra, the girl who had been outside the school crying on the day when this had all started. Tierra, who had later assured me that her sadness had nothing to do with the cheating accusations.

Was "Sick&Tired" Tierra? I couldn't know for sure, but I thought of all the things I'd seen on her page. People had attacked the way she looked, the way she talked—almost everything about her. Plus, I knew she was sensitive to things, and she'd been acting so weird lately. . . .

I pulled up her Instagram. She was one of those Instagrammers who posted memes all the time. I saw that there were some funny ones, but those were from weeks before. Lately she'd just been posting sad quotes. Right before that, the quotes had been confidence-boosting ones like, *If people are talking about you, they're just jealous.* But the past dozen or so were about how sad, lonely, and lost a person could feel.

It was her. I just *knew* it.

Once I'd made that decision, I knew exactly what I had to do. I couldn't wait for school Monday. I couldn't even wait for Janelle to help. I had to go find Tierra.

And I knew exactly where she'd be.

CHAPTER 11

We talked my dad into taking us to find Tierra.
Only, he didn't know why we were going. All he knew was
that we needed to go to the church to help out with something. The church where Tierra and I had spent every
Saturday afternoon back when we were BFFs.

The price of our ride to that church? A trip down mem-
ory lane with Dad.

"Do you remember that time we stopped for chocolate-
dipped ice cream and Tierra dropped hers?" he asked. "My
brand-new car."

He shook his head. I looked back over my shoulder at Janelle. She was staring down at her phone.

"She still hasn't texted back," Janelle said. "Maybe we should stop by her house. She could help us."

Janelle had been texting Adria for the past couple of hours, with no response at all. She'd even tried to video-chat her. Nothing but silence. She probably was out with her parents or something. No big deal. But Janelle was getting that wrinkle between her eyebrows that she always got when she was worried.

"Then how will we get to the church?" I asked. My dad was going straight to the office after dropping us off.

"Good point," Janelle said, distracted.

"Here we are," Dad said, flipping on his right turn signal and turning into the church. "Just text when you need us to come get you."

"Or we'll call my mom," Janelle said. "Maybe we can go to Adria's house?"

I looked back at Janelle again. She definitely was concerned about Adria. Which was weird. Normally she'd be more annoyed than worried. I wondered if they'd gotten into a fight or something. Or maybe this

SlamBook stuff was just messing with all of us.

"Thanks," I said, hopping out of the car and shoving my phone into my back pocket. I couldn't really put serious time into worrying about Adria now. If Tierra really was Sick&Tired, we had big, big problems to solve.

"What if she isn't here?" Janelle asked as we approached the ginormous front door to the church.

It felt like it had been eons since I'd been there. But it was almost automatic to walk in, turn immediately to the right, and take the stairs behind the door by the long table where they had coffee and pastries on Sunday morning. Even the smell—fresh paint mixed with a disinfectant sort of hospital scent—was as familiar as if I'd climbed these steps the day before.

I didn't answer Janelle's question. Truth was, I hadn't thought about Tierra not being at the church. I was that sure she'd stuck to our old tradition, even if there were things going on in her life that would make her upset. She never missed this.

Once we reached the top of the steps, I pulled the door open, wincing at the loud squeal it made. It seemed as loud as a clap of thunder in the way-too-quiet building. At any minute, I expected some security guard to come running toward us, demanding to know why we were there, but I'd never seen any sign of security in all the times I'd been there. Besides, we weren't doing anything wrong, anyway. We were looking for our classmate.

"This is creepy," Janelle commented as we walked down the long corridor. The tiles were some weird green-gray color that matched the stripe that ran all the way along the walls. The place just seemed so clean and perfect.

"It's all the way at the end," I said. But we should have been hearing something by then, right? What if they'd moved? It had been a few months. Things couldn't possibly have changed that quickly, could they?

Just as I was starting to doubt my decision to drag Janelle here, though, I heard it. The faint, faraway sounds of people chatting. And in between the chatter, I could hear the light sound of music. It all got clearer and louder as we walked.

"Wait!" Janelle whispered, reaching out to touch my arm to stop me. "What's the plan?"

Oh. Good question. Once I'd figured out that Tierra was Sick&Tired, the only thing on my mind had been to track her down and talk to her. That was it. I felt like I had to get to her as quickly as possible. But if she was here, doing her Saturday thing, she wasn't in immediate danger.

Maybe we needed a different plan.

"We can't confront her," I said. "Not here. But I think we can help her. Just follow me."

Janelle had a puzzled look, but I felt like instinct would guide me on what to do next. Yes, I needed to talk to Tierra about this, but not with Janelle standing there too. That would never work. The second she saw Janelle, she'd clam up.

I walked with purpose straight toward the room at the end of the hall. I was so sure of myself. But once I got to the doorway and looked into the room, my confidence wavered.

The room was far fuller than I remembered, with every seat filled. There were four-seater tables crammed into the room, with barely enough space to walk in between each one. Elderly people, mostly women, were seated at the tables, staring intently down at the cards they were holding. Then there was the *clink-clink-clink* of poker chips. All around the room were people our age and slightly older, leaning over shoulders and helping the players who needed it.

"There she is," Janelle said, pointing toward the back corner.

Sure enough, Tierra stood behind a woman who seemed to be having trouble holding her cards in place. Tierra kept reaching down to pull them up so that other people at the table wouldn't see them.

"Okay, everyone," a woman standing scarily close to us shouted. "This is your last hand. Make it count."

"What is this?" Janelle whispered.

"Senior game day," I said. "Three to five, every Saturday."

"Huh." Janelle commented, still taking it all in.

But my attention was mostly focused on Tierra, who seemed to have spotted us. She was staring at us from her hunched-over position, her eyes slightly squinted as if she couldn't quite make us out. Or maybe what she couldn't make out was why we were there.

I had a plan for that, though.

I stepped into the room and moved off to the side, to the corner where there was a row of chairs lined up against the wall. I gestured for Janelle to follow, but she didn't at first. Not until I was seated. Then, looking around as if she felt totally out of place, she crept over to where I was sitting and plopped down next to me.

"What's the plan here?" she asked.

Luckily, nobody else seemed to have noticed we were there. No surprise. These games could get pretty intense, I remembered. Even the volunteers had a hard time keeping up. We could probably have sat there the whole two hours without anyone even seeing us.

Finally, after what seemed like forever, everyone started moving at once, with the woman yelling instructions about where to leave their chips and cards. I stood, and Janelle immediately stood as well. I wasn't sure what Tierra would do, now that she'd seen us. If she tried to escape without talking to us, it wouldn't surprise me, especially since she'd probably noticed Janelle.

As we were pushing our way toward the middle of the room, Tierra suddenly appeared through a split in the crowd, walking straight toward us. She was frowning as she looked from me to Janelle and back again.

"Is something wrong?" she asked.

Oh! She probably thought we'd been sent to find her

with some sort of bad news. But what bad news would we have? Did she think we were coming to talk to her about SlamBook or something? Maybe that was it.

"Do you have plans for tonight?" I asked her, trying to sound as legit as possible. We had to make her believe we'd come here specifically for this purpose.

"No," she said hesitantly. Now she was looking at just me. I didn't blame her. I was also afraid to see what Janelle's reaction to this would be. Maybe I should have warned Janelle somehow, but I was just going on instinct here. I hadn't meant to ask if she had plans tonight, or to invite her over to my house. I just felt like we needed a reason for showing up here all of a sudden.

"We're doing a sleepover at my house," I said. "We want you to come too. *I* want you to come too."

Now she looked at Janelle. I knew by the way her lips pursed together just a tiny, tiny bit that she was skeptical. She wanted to know what we were up to. She probably thought we were going to do that thing where we tried to make her think she was popular so that we could play some horrible prank on her.

"We're brainstorming how to fix the whole SlamBook

thing," I blurted out. Yes, that was part of the plan that had been churning around in my brain for the past ten minutes or so. "I loved what you said at the library that day. I think you can help."

I wasn't going to mention Sick&Tired, but I'd assumed this would be the point when I'd know for sure that Tierra was behind that comment. She'd make a face or something. But she didn't. She still had that skeptical-confused look.

"We're having pizza," Janelle said cheerily from behind me.

I turned to look at her, figuring I'd see a different person there. Someone who maybe sounded just like Janelle but looked like someone else entirely. Because no way would the Janelle I knew (a) be *that* cheerful about pizza, or (b) want Tierra to hang out with us.

Nope, same Janelle. Only, the smile on her face was joined by something else in her eyes. Pity? Concern? I wasn't sure what to call it exactly, but it was anything but excitement about a fun sleepover with Tierra Ford.

"Oh . . . o-kay," Tierra said, and I flipped around to face her again. Tierra had the opposite expression. She was frowning and confused, but there was a glimmer of some-thing in her eyes. Was it . . . excitement?

Yes, excitement.

That made every single bit of this worth it. Whether Janelle liked it or not, this was definitely the right thing to do. Including Tierra in our plans could make a 100 percent difference.

Plus, a part of me was also excited to get to hang out with Tierra again. Maybe I could do something to make up for the crappy way I'd treated her.

CHAPTER 12

"Please, please, please, *please*?"

Yes, it had come to this. I was begging. I'd get down on my knees if I had to. Whatever it took to convince Mom to let me have a sleepover that night.

I guess I should have thought this through a little better. When I'd come up with my last-minute plan to save Tierra from the brink of suicide, I hadn't actually considered how I'd handle it with my parents. I had never had a sleepover before, so I wasn't even sure what the protocol was in my house. Hope had one or two friends over sometimes, but three?

"You just can't spring something like this on us at the last minute," Mom said. "There's planning involved."

"No planning," I said. "We'll order some super cheap pizzas from that place down the street, and everyone will sleep in my room."

"You just had pizza last night," Mom said, as though that was relevant at all. She knew I could eat pizza every night. Maybe even for every *meal*.

"I'll get different toppings," I said with a shrug. "It'll be like a totally different meal."

"You have a twin bed," Mom pointed out. "There's not enough room for three air mattresses on your floor."

"They can sleep on blankets," I said. "My floor's carpeted. It's not like they'll be sleeping on *this* floor."

I pointed down to the hardwood flooring that was in every room of our house but the bedrooms. I wasn't sure how Janelle and Adria would feel about sleeping on carpet, but I was pretty sure Tierra would be fine with it. She was easygoing about things like that—another reason I missed having her as a friend.

"And what about breakfast in the morning?" Mom asked.

"Cereal's fine," I said. "We're not fancy."

"She's never had a sleepover," Dad chimed in. He'd been sitting over in his recliner, staring at his phone during the whole discussion until now.

I wanted to hug Dad for saying that, even though he still hadn't looked up from his screen. All that was left was for Mom to give in.

This had been the hardest part. If I could have told her the truth about why I wanted a sleepover, it would have been easier. Or maybe not. I didn't want to even mention that Tierra was having problems lately and I wanted to include her. I feared that things would be awkward when she showed up. She needed to feel like nothing at all was wrong.

Mom not only okayed the sleepover, but she promised to stop by the grocery store on the way back from dropping Hope off at her friend's. Hope, in the meantime, had asked seven times, "You are having a sleepover? *You?*"

"Yes, me," I said. And then I gave her my stare of death, as if to say, *Do you want to make something of it?*

"Stay out of my room," she said, tossing her hair back over her shoulder as she pranced out the door.

I just rolled my eyes and looked back at my phone screen. Janelle was on her way, but she was stopping by to get Adria first. Now they were in the car and I was getting a play-by-play of everything Adria was and was *not* doing.

Janelle: **She's staring at her phone. Why?**

Me: **Aren't you staring at yours?**

Janelle: **Yes, but still . . .**

Janelle was being a little too obsessive about this whole Adria thing. It wasn't like Adria had never been moody before. But maybe Janelle had never seen this side of her?

Me: **Did you tell her Tierra's coming?**

A long time passed. Too long. I was starting to wonder if maybe I'd lost her. And then I saw the three dots that indicated she was typing something.

Janelle: **I just told her.**

Another long pause. No dots. I shook my phone in frustration. She was obviously trying to make me lose my mind.

Me: **And?**

Janelle: **Nothing.**

Me: **What do you mean?**

Janelle: **She said nothing. Didn't even shrug???**

Well, maybe that was a good thing. At least she wasn't

throwing a fit about it. She very easily could have insisted that Janelle's dad take her home immediately. Instead she was acting like she didn't care. Maybe she had something going on, like a crush on someone.

Or it could be a SlamBook thing. I hadn't even checked her page recently. Was there something really horrible on there and she just didn't want to talk about it? Maybe she'd tell us that night.

Me: **Have you checked her page recently?**

Janelle: **SlamBook?**

I rolled my eyes. Of course, SlamBook. What other "page" would she have?

Me: **Yes. I don't want to look. Can you?**

Janelle: **Hold on.**

It was funny. Just a couple of days before, I would have rushed right to her page, eager to see what I'd missed. Now I couldn't even bring myself to look. I was almost . . . scared of it? I didn't want to look at the main page comments, either, just in case it had gotten worse. Now that I knew Tierra was Sick&Tired, there was no mystery to solve. No reason to look at SlamBook, except for my own curiosity.

Janelle: **Looks the same as before.**

I breathed a sigh of relief. But that did nothing to solve the mystery of what was wrong with Adria. There had to be something she wasn't telling us about. Something she'd tell us about that night?

Ha! Not with Tierra there, she wouldn't.

When the doorbell rang, my heart started racing. I couldn't explain why either. All we had to really do was make sure Tierra felt included. But I couldn't guarantee that Adria would do that, especially since Janelle hadn't clued her in to what was really going on. I was guessing that Adria hadn't even asked why she was being driven to a sleepover at my house. I could see Janelle's point. Adria was not herself.

I opened the door hesitantly, expecting to find Janelle and Adria on the other side. Instead it was Tierra. She still had that same mixture of confusion and disguised excitement on her face.

"Come in," I said. "Oh, you brought a sleeping bag."

She looked down at the large blue bag that had the words "Sleeping Bag" on a label toward the top.

"Is that Tierra?" Mom asked from behind me. "Hi, sweetie. I've missed you."

I held in a gasp. *Mom.* Ugh. Did she have to call attention to the fact that Tierra hadn't been to the house in a while?

"Hi, Mrs. Taylor," Tierra said quietly.

"Come on in," Mom said. "Faith's dad has gone to get the pizzas, but in the meantime we have all kinds of snacks. Faith, do you want to show her where she'll be sleeping?"

Not really. That meant being alone with her. And I wasn't sure what to do once I had her alone. I was kind of hoping Janelle would have figured that part out.

What did you do when you knew someone was upset to the point of being suicidal? I had no idea. There was a phone number she could call, and I could Google that, but Tierra wasn't exactly asking us for help. We weren't even supposed to know she was upset. She'd probably be mortified if she found out I knew she was Sick&Tired.

Make her feel included. Part of the group. Make her see that there were people who liked her, and what some jerks had posted on SlamBook was no big deal when compared to that. Those were the only things we could do right then, and if that didn't work, we could refer her to someone who could help her. We'd get the school counselor involved—or

179

my parents, if it seemed like we couldn't wait until Monday.

"We'll be sleeping in my room," I said as we walked upstairs. "We have a bunch of blankets and pillows and stuff that you can use with your sleeping bag. Do you use one pillow or two? Because I only use one, but my sister always has to have two, which is a total pain when we're staying at hotels and stuff, you know?"

I realized even as I was doing it that I was babbling. Just talking away, as I did when I got nervous. But I didn't want Tierra to know I was nervous. I took deep breaths to try to calm myself down.

"Why did you invite me here?"

We'd reached the top of the stairs when Tierra asked that question. In fact, I stumbled on the top step in my surprise. I hadn't expected her to be so blunt. And, of course, I had no answer whatsoever prepared for that question.

I stalled by going to the bedroom, waiting for her to come in, and shutting the door behind us. I still wasn't sure what to say, but I was hoping something would come to me in the moments it took to walk to my bed and sit down on the corner of it.

My laptop, lying in the center of the bed where I'd left

it after reading Sick&Tired's comment, inspired me. I decided to go with semi-honesty.

"Janelle and I are just sick of all the SlamBook stuff," I said. "It's gone too far. So we've made a pact. No more checking it. No more leaving comments. We're done. This sleepover is a celebration of our decision to do that. Are you in?"

She shrugged. "Sure. No big deal. I haven't really been following it at all. It's kind of silly, really."

I didn't respond at first, mostly because I was speechless. I wasn't sure what I might have predicted she'd say, but this wasn't it. I didn't know how to respond.

Was she lying? Maybe she knew we'd read the Sick&Tired comment and she was trying to pretend none of it mattered to her. Because no way would she have written that comment and not have reacted to what I'd said.

"Have you left any slams?" I asked her.

"I don't have an account," she said. "My parents have one of those blocks on our internet. I looked at my page a while ago from the library, but it's just too much trouble. I don't care what people say about me."

OMG. She seemed like she was telling the truth. I

couldn't see even a hint in her expression that she might have been hiding that she was active on SlamBook. And I did remember how weird her mom had always been about screen time. Tierra hadn't even been allowed to watch TV for more than two hours a day. But I didn't know anything about a block on her internet.

"There was this comment," I said as Tierra wandered around the room, looking at the pictures I had on my bulletin board and dresser. Most of them were of family, but there were a few of me and Janelle and one with Adria. I felt a pang of guilt as she browsed past those. "It was on the main page."

"Oh?" she asked. She sounded so disinterested, I wondered if she'd even heard me.

"The person was really upset," I said. "She even threatened suicide."

That got Tierra's attention. She turned around, her mouth frozen in an O shape.

"Yeah," I said. "So we're not only boycotting the page, but we're also trying to figure out who posted the comment."

"You said it's a 'she,'" she said, pulling the chair away

from my desk and turning it so it faced me. Then she sat down. "How do you know that?"

I opened my mouth to answer, but then closed it again. Had I said it was a she? If so, I hadn't even realized it. But now that she mentioned it, I *had* been assuming Sick&Tired was a girl. There was no legit reason it couldn't be a guy.

Great. Now it would be even harder to pinpoint exactly who this person was. It could literally be anyone at school. *Anyone.*

"Read it to me," Tierra said.

"Are you sure?" I asked.

She nodded. I opened my laptop, navigated to the main page comments screen, and read every word of Sick&Tired's post. If there had been even a small amount of suspicion left that Tierra had written this, it was gone as Tierra listened, fascinated, while I read.

"Wow," she said when I was finished. "That's serious."

"I know," I said. "How could we possibly have even seen signs that someone was this upset?"

"There's, like, a billion people at school," she said. "How many of them have SlamBook accounts?"

I shook my head. "Most of them?" I asked.

"And you can't possibly have looked at every SlamBook page."

"No way." I laughed. "There aren't enough hours in the day."

Even if I could have looked at every single page, I wouldn't have wanted to. Mostly I'd focused on people I knew, and I knew nothing about pages outside of our grade. There were just too many people.

"You can just hack into it and find out, can't you?" she asked. "Maybe ask Ms. Wang?"

I stared at her a minute. Right. She knew about Ms. Wang—I had mentioned my coding club before we had stopped hanging out—so Tierra must have known a little about it.

"If anyone can figure all this out, you can," Tierra said. "You're supersmart. I was surprised you and Janelle—"

"What?" I asked.

"Nothing," she said, shaking her head. "Never mind."

I knew what she'd been about to say. Janelle and I weren't exactly a "fit" personality-wise. Janelle was into things that I'd never shown an interest in before hanging out with her. I'd always thought it was a good idea to have friends who brought out different sides of you, but I'd underestimated how good it might feel to have a friend I could share my love for coding with.

"Hey!"

The sound of Janelle's voice made me jump. I'd been so focused on my conversation with Tierra, I hadn't even noticed her standing in the doorway. I backtracked to what we'd said just before, worried she might have heard something. If she had, though, it didn't show on her face.

"Are we late?" Janelle asked, entering the room to make way for Adria, who moved into the doorway behind her. Adria already looked bored.

"Not at all," I said. "I was just catching Tierra up on things."

Janelle's reaction to that was an expression of surprise mixed with confusion. I remembered then. Janelle had no idea that I'd figured out that Tierra wasn't Sick&Tired. I had to find a way to get Janelle alone to tell her what Tierra and I had just discussed.

Then I thought, *Or maybe I should just say it now, outright.* Where everyone could hear. Then we could spend the rest of the night trying to figure it all out.

"Pizza's here!" Mom called from downstairs, interrupting any hope I had of bringing the subject of Sick&Tired up immediately. I'd just have to figure out a way to make it part of the discussion after dinner, since I couldn't mention SlamBook with Mom around.

Adria led the way downstairs, with Janelle behind her, chattering all the way about how she'd just found her favorite lip balm online somewhere. I glanced back at Tierra, who rolled her eyes, making me suppress a laugh. Then I felt guilty for being part of making fun of Janelle. But she was seriously fixated on the wrong things. Especially with all that was going on right then.

My eyes widened when I entered the kitchen to see what Mom had done. Pizzas lined the counters—more pizzas than there were people. Plus, there were cupcakes, chips and salsa, and my favorite—California rolls. I wanted to hug Mom in thanks, but she'd waved good-bye on her way out the door as we'd come down the stairs. Dad was waiting in the car to take her to dinner. We were on our own . . . for a little while, anyway.

Janelle grabbed a plate and headed straight to the California rolls. Adria trailed along behind her, still quiet. Tierra and I headed for the extra-meaty pizza on the end.

"Is there vegetarian?" Adria asked.

They were the first words she'd said all night. Tierra pointed out the cheese and veggie pizzas that were close to where they stood, and Adria added a slice to her plate.

"You missed all the fun today," I told Adria once we were seated. "We got to go to the church and watch seniors play poker."

I was basically trying to make conversation to pull Adria out of her shell. Which was weird, since she'd never been in that shell before. She'd always just jumped right into whatever situation was in front of her. In fact, she'd normally be the one talking our ears off. Was it because Tierra was there? Maybe she and Janelle had had words about it in the car on the way over or something.

But that didn't explain why she hadn't answered Janelle's texts earlier that day. I would have to ask Janelle what was going on with that.

"Yeah, what's that all about?" Janelle asked Tierra.

"Is your grandmother there or something?"

"I've been helping out at the church since I was in second grade," Tierra said with a shrug. "My parents think it's good for me to get involved."

That was pretty much what she'd told me when we used to hang out together. And I had to admit, helping out on Saturdays had been enjoyable, and only partly because we'd always stopped for ice cream afterward. After just one time, I'd started looking forward to it. Those old people were so much fun!

"Doesn't it kind of suck to have to hang out there every Saturday?" Janelle asked.

"No," Tierra said. "Why would it?"

She was giving Janelle a challenging look, and not backing down. The air shifted around us as we watched the silent interaction. Suddenly the bite of pizza I'd taken sat like a lump in my stomach.

"I don't know," Janelle finally said. "I just thought maybe you'd want to do other things. Like go to the movies or hang out with friends."

I searched my mind desperately for a way to change the subject. I decided to dive in.

"So . . . I told Tierra about the comment from Sick&Tired," I blurted. "She hasn't been spending much time on SlamBook lately."

Janelle turned to stare at me. She seemed to be giving me some kind of silent message in that look. I tried to send a silent message back, but when that didn't work, I used words.

"She was shocked to hear about the whole thing," I said. "She couldn't believe someone had written that."

"It's all so horrible," Tierra said, shaking her head. "We have to figure out who Sick&Tired is."

"It's disgusting," Adria blurted.

Her tone was so harsh, it startled me. I blinked at her in surprise. For someone who'd barely said anything all night, those words were a shocker. She hadn't even looked up from the slice of pizza on her plate. She was methodically picking off every single onion and setting it aside.

"What's disgusting?" Janelle asked in a strangely sweet tone. Like she was afraid Adria might get mean if she wasn't careful.

"We're all at the same school," she said. "Isn't there any such thing as school loyalty? School *pride*?"

I frowned. There was something about that comment that sounded really familiar. . . .

"You think gossiping about other people is betraying your school somehow?" Tierra asked. "Even the cheerleaders gossip."

I frowned as I chomped on my pizza. Janelle wasn't used to having people push back on her. And she was also a cheerleader, to boot!

To my surprise, Janelle just laughed. "She's right about that," Janelle said. "You can have school pride and still gossip. You're gossiping about the people in the school."

"It's like talking about your family," Tierra added excitedly. "You can do it, but if other people do it, you get mad."

"Exactly," Janelle said.

I couldn't believe Janelle and Tierra were actually getting along. It sounded almost like they were bonding. And Adria wasn't participating at all. She was tearing small pieces of her pizza off and stacking them on her plate. Had she even eaten a bite? And why was something bugging me?

We share the same school pride.

I knew immediately what had been bugging me. *Adria* was Sick&Tired.

CHAPTER 13

The words hit me all at once. They were so powerful, I had to hold myself back from saying them out loud. They had been in the opening paragraph of Sick&Tired's long, long comment. They'd stuck out to me as odd when I'd first read them too. Like, what did school pride have to do with gossip?

"I just think we should stick together, that's all," Adria said. "It's all so mean."

"That's why I don't participate," Tierra said. "Unplugging is the most freeing thing you can do. Just step away from the screen and do something else."

"Once you've read it, it gets in here," Adria said, pointing to her head. "And that's where it stays."

I opened my mouth to say something, then closed it again. I looked at Janelle and Tierra. Neither one of them seemed to have figured out what had finally hit me, and why would they? It had taken me several minutes to place where I'd heard the words before.

The worst part was, I couldn't say anything right then. I had to figure out what I was supposed to do about this. I could talk to Adria directly, but what would I say? I could talk to Janelle, but it would be hard for me to get her to believe me. Tierra was the best option. I had to get Tierra alone.

I had my chance when we were putting the pizzas away. Janelle and Adria decided that was the very minute to carry their overnight bags up to my bedroom. They'd left them in the living room for some reason. As they creaked their way up the stairs, I grabbed Tierra's arm with the hand that wasn't holding a dish towel.

"It's Adria," I said. "Adria is Sick&Tired."

I could tell that Tierra wasn't quite getting what I was saying. She probably had already forgotten the username of the person who had left the comment on SlamBook. I was guessing that at first she thought I was saying Adria was actually "sick and tired" of something.

"The comment on SlamBook?" I reminded her. "It started out talking about how people should have too much school pride to be mean to each other. That was pretty much exactly what Adria said, right?"

"Oh!" Tierra said. She turned and looked in the direction Janelle and Adria had headed. They were still upstairs, I assumed. "So . . . Adria?"

"Adria," I said.

And that was when it sank in for the first time. Adria had been really affected by the horrible slams on her page. I couldn't blame her. They were super personal, both the racist ones and the ones that attacked her appearance. Her slams had been the reason why I'd wanted to take revenge on the people writing horrible things.

"What are we going to do?" Tierra asked.

I set the dish towel down and switched to consolidating the leftover pizza into a couple of boxes. I honestly didn't know the answer to that. I'd been hoping Tierra would.

stop hanging out with me if they knew I was really, really into coding. I don't know why."

But I did know why. Even now, I could picture Janelle with her excitement over lip balm realizing that we really didn't have all that much in common, after all. And then she would stop hanging out with me and I'd go right back to being invisible.

"Who cares how they see it, anyway?" Tierra asked. "It's you. It's who you are. Why are you pretending it's not a thing?"

"I'm not," I said. "It just . . . never came up."

"Well, guess what?" Tierra asked. "It has now. If you don't want to tell them, I can."

I shook my head. The last thing I wanted was for Tierra to give them a reason to be mad at her. This was 100 percent on me.

She was right. It was time.

I took a deep breath, flipped around, and opened the door. I walked quickly and with purpose. If I was going to do this, I had to do it before I changed my mind.

"I'm in a computer programming club," I blurted as soon as I walked through the door.

Only after the words were out did I realize that Janelle was sitting there alone.

"Where's Adria?" I asked. The plan had been to disclose this to both of them, not just one. I didn't want to have to go through this explanation twice.

"She left," Janelle said. "What do you mean, computer programming club? Like, you're learning to program computers or something?"

"Yes," I said. "But wait. She left? She went home?"

"Yes," she said. "She wasn't feeling well. That's what she said, anyway."

"I don't understand," I said.

Not only was this derailing the whole conversation I'd psyched myself up to have, but it was throwing me for a loop. How were we going to address the whole Sick&Tired thing if Adria was gone?

"Something's not right with her," Janelle said.

I shook my head. Way too much was going on. First things first.

"I've been learning how to code," I said. "Computer programming. Just what you said a second ago. And when SlamBook came along, I used what I'd learned to examine the site's source code and figure out who had posted what. It's . . . complicated, but that's how I knew."

She set my laptop aside and clasped her hands on her lap in front of her. "So you posted mean comments to get back at people for what you found that they'd written?" she asked.

I nodded. And waited for her to get mad. Or to judge me. Or whatever it was I'd been expecting her to do. She did none of that, though. Instead she just stared thoughtfully into space.

"That makes sense," she said. "So, what about Adria?"

"We think she's Sick&Tired," Tierra said from the doorway.

I didn't know how long she'd been standing there, listening, but I was glad she had been. My brain was still scrambled from the drama I'd just gone through. And there were things much, much, *much* more important to deal with right then.

"Wait . . . what?" Janelle asked. "What do you mean? She can't be."

"Well, we aren't one hundred percent sure," I said. "She said something tonight that was straight out of Sick&Tired's comment."

"The part about school pride," Tierra said.

"Let me read it again." Janelle grabbed my laptop and navigated to the main comments page. She reread the whole comment aloud, her voice getting slower and draggier as she went. I could tell she was hearing the words in Adria's voice. She was thinking of them from the perspective of the girl who had been her best friend for years.

"You're right," she said as soon as the last words of the comment were out of her mouth. "That's Adria, right?"

"But what if it's not?" I asked. I would feel even worse if I'd been wrong about the whole thing, especially if we said something to her specifically.

"We'll wade in slowly," Janelle said. "Feel her out. If it seems like she isn't Sick&Tired, we'll bail. Right?"

She looked at both me and Tierra. Did that mean we were all three going to handle this together? As a team?

"Okay," I said. "But we need a plan."

CHAPTER 14

"Hel-*lo*. Earth to Faith."

I didn't realize until I heard my name that I'd zoned out midbreakfast. It had been a rough Sunday. Pretty much the roughest Sunday of my life. I'd spent the day going back and forth between Janelle and Tierra on text, just trying to figure out what we could do to fix this mess.

And now it was Monday morning. The plan was set. We'd go to school and track Adria down. We'd get her alone somewhere and have a talk with her. I hadn't really wanted to wait a full day, but Tierra had pointed out that if we were at school, we could get the guidance counselor involved if we had to. Even if it meant blowing SlamBook out of the water.

But also, there had been no easy way to explain to my mom that we all needed a ride to Adria's house. I'd called in all my parental favors with my sleepover the night before, and I didn't want to push things. Plus, we couldn't seem to agree on whether it was a good or bad idea to talk to Adria when her parents were around.

"Sorry," I said, returning my attention to my cereal with renewed enthusiasm. Well, *pretend* renewed enthusiasm, anyway. It was just me and Hope right then. Dad had taken a rideshare to the airport for his business trip.

"It's that website, isn't it?" Hope asked.

My head snapped up, the cereal in my mouth suddenly feeling like a pile of rocks. I chewed quickly and swallowed.

"What did you say?" I asked.

"That SlamBook site. Or is it an app? I don't know the difference. I think apps have to be downloaded, though, don't they?"

I just stared. Had the word "SlamBook" really just come out of Hope's mouth?

"Everyone's been talking about it," she said. "Do you think I'm the only one with a little sister in middle school? Seriously. Everyone's freaking out."

"How long have you known about it?" I asked her.

"Few days," she said with a shrug. "I figured you would've mentioned it if you were worried about it. But you've been acting weirder than usual lately. I mean, a sleepover? Really?"

"What does that have to do with SlamBook?" I asked.

"I don't know," she said. "I figured maybe SlamBook was messing with your mind so much, you had to get away from it and do a sleepover."

She wasn't wrong about that. But it was much more complicated. There wasn't enough time to tell her everything that was happening. But it would feel so good to talk to her.

"Did you hear about the comment someone left on the main page for our school?" I whispered.

"No," she said.

"Look it up," I said. "It was really bad."

Mom came in before I could say anything else. But

I could see Hope eyeing her phone as she chomped her cereal and answered Mom's questions.

"I'll drop you both off at school," Mom said. "My morning class was canceled."

That sounded perfect. I wasn't really in the mood to sit on the bus, listening to everyone chatter on about nothing important. I'd just feel much better once I was at school with my friends and could see that everything was okay with Adria and do something about it if it wasn't. Until then, I would remain a big bundle of nerves.

My phone buzzed in my back pocket, and I had to force myself to ignore it. Janelle had been updating me on the previous night's convo with Adria. Everything had seemed fine then. Janelle seemed to think we'd be safe to wait to talk to her at school.

I hadn't been so sure about that, but I hadn't been able to come up with a way around it.

"I thought maybe we could all go out to dinner tonight," Mom said. "Just the three of us. A girls' night."

Mom was so cheerful and casual, it felt out of place. Not that she wasn't always cheerful and casual. It just didn't seem right that day. Everyone should have been anguished and frowny.

"Sounds good," I said, taking my bowl to the sink to rinse it out. My phone buzzed again, and I spun around so that the screen would be facing away from my mom and sister when I read what was on it.

Janelle: **Adria's not here.**

I stared at the screen, for the first few seconds not quite comprehending what I was seeing. *Not here*? What did that mean?

Me: **Not where?**

I pretty much knew the answer before she typed it. There was a sinking feeling in the pit of my stomach. This was not good. Not good at all.

Janelle: **At school. She's not answering her phone either.**

That last part was no surprise, but I'd expected her to be at school. She had to be at school. If she wasn't at school, something could be very, very wrong.

"Faith?"

Mom's voice seemed like it was coming from far away.

I leaned back against the sink and looked up from the screen. Both Mom and Hope were staring at me, concern etched on their faces.

"What's going on?" Mom asked.

I burst into tears.

Not tears welling in my eyes and gently spilling over. Full-on *tears*, complete with me sobbing and covering my face with the hand that wasn't holding my phone. It was like all the tears I'd cry for the rest of my life had been stored up in my body for the past couple of days and had suddenly been set free. Once I started crying, there was no way I could stop.

"Faith!" Mom blurted, rushing over to me. I felt her arms around me and gave in to her hug. No matter what happened in life, nothing felt better than your mom's hug.

I knew that at some point I'd have to explain why I was crying. I didn't want to do that. But inevitably Mom started pulling back, and I had to face it. I had to face her.

"My friend Adria," I said. "She's not at school today. We're worried about her."

"Okay, well, have you tried calling her?"

Mom looked over at Hope, who had now moved closer and was staring at me. She was giving me a look. It was like she was just bursting to shout, "Tell her!"

"Yes," I said. "Janelle has. Plus, there's . . . more."

I was looking at Hope as though she could help me or something. But I needed to do this. I needed to just open up to my mom. I should have done it days before.

"There's this website," I said. "It's called SlamBook. People write mean things about each other. Someone left a comment, and we think we've tracked it to Adria. It was . . . well, it seemed like whoever it was might do something horrible."

"She might hurt herself," Hope said.

"What?" Mom asked. "Why on Earth—?"

"It got pretty ugly," I said. "I should have told you. Or we should have told some adult. At first we didn't want the site taken down, but then we did but things had gone way too far."

"We have to call the police," Mom said, crossing the kitchen to the coat hooks, which was where she always hung her purse. "We'll tell them to go check on her. They do wellness checks all the time."

"No!" I yelled.

I hadn't meant to shout that. Calling the police probably was the right thing to do, but what if we were wrong? What if Adria was just home sick or something?

"We can go by her house," I said. "Can you take me to her house?"

Mom looked stunned. Dazed. It was pretty much how I'd felt all weekend.

"Yes," Mom said. "Let's go."

CHAPTER 15

I leapt out of Mom's SUV as soon as it rolled to a stop in Adria's driveway. Then I ran straight for the door.

I heard footsteps on the walkway behind me as I climbed the steps to the front porch. It was either Mom or Hope. Didn't matter which. I was set on my destination. I punched the doorbell and banged on the door with my fist as hard as I could, just in case the doorbell wasn't working.

The problem was, I hadn't thought through what I was going to say once that door opened. I just knew I had to do something. I had to talk to her before my mom called the police and made a big scene. I had to make sure everything was okay.

"Nobody's answering," Hope said. "I'm calling the police."

"Hold on," I said, turning the doorknob. I was desperate at that point. Something told me I did not want the police to show up. Something told me I needed to get inside.

The doorknob turned freely. The door creaked open. What? Who left the front door just unlocked in this town?

Someone who didn't care if a burglar broke in.

I looked back at Hope, whose eyes were wide. In my peripheral vision I could see Mom coming up the walk behind her. She'd try to stop me. Tell me I needed to wait and let her go in first. Since we'd left the house, she'd been arguing that she should go in instead of me.

Knowing Mom might stop me was all I needed to push me to move. I entered the house, not worrying about whether the front door was closed behind me or Hope followed me or Mom followed me or anything else. I was on a mission. I had to get to Adria's bedroom and figure out what was going on.

The house seemed eerily quiet. And empty. I knew her parents worked, and it was getting later in the morning, but would they have just left her alone? Didn't they know something was wrong with Adria?

Or maybe they did know. Had something happened? I shuddered at the thought.

My heart was pounding as I walked down the hallway toward Adria's bedroom. I'd only been here a few times— always trailing along after Janelle. In truth, I had rarely spent time alone with Adria, and now was going to be one of those rare instances. It seemed wrong. But I didn't have time to wait for Janelle to help me.

"Is she in there?"

I barely stopped a shriek from escaping when Hope bumped into me. I'd come to a sudden stop in front of Adria's closed bedroom door, not sure what I'd see on the other side of it. But having Hope beside me gave me more courage than I would have had alone.

As I put my hand on the knob and turned it clockwise, I half expected it to not budge at all. It would be locked,

I was sure, and then I'd have no idea what to do. But, surprisingly, it turned easily, and with a loud click the door started to slide inward.

Until I saw Adria, I hadn't really thought through what I might find. I'd just had this huge sense of urgency to get to her house, combined with a dread of what I'd see when I did. But it didn't surprise me at all to find Adria in bed. I could see her form as a lump beneath the sheets. She was on her side. I held my breath, creeping into her bedroom.

That was when Adria moved. And I let out my breath in a huge sigh of relief.

"Adria?" I asked.

Everything was still for a moment. But then she moved. She turned her head and looked at me. And said, in a raspy voice, "What are you doing here?"

"You weren't at school," I said.

I didn't dare creep any closer. And I wasn't sure what had happened to Hope and my mom, but I didn't want to move. I just assumed they were out there in the hall, waiting in case I needed them.

"I'm not feeling well," she said, pushing her covers down and scooting up a little. That elevated her head some more, which also showed me that she'd been crying. Her eyes were red and puffy, and her complexion was bright red. Any other time, I'd pretend I didn't notice. There was too much at stake, though.

"You've been crying," I said. "And I bet you've been crying about SlamBook."

She shook her head and pursed her lips stubbornly. But tears were pooling in her eyes. No matter what, she couldn't keep those tears back.

"It's bigger than SlamBook, though," I said, going with my gut. "It's the way you feel at school every day. The people looking at you. You knowing what they wrote. You assume everyone feels the way that mean commenter felt, but you know what? That's not true."

"You don't know me," she snapped. "You don't know anything."

She was right. I thought back to the racist comment she'd received. Yes, I'd also gotten some nasty remarks, but I couldn't possibly know—and honestly, would never know—how it felt to be judged for where my parents were from. I didn't have to worry about people thinking I didn't belong here. "I know how much those comments hurt."

"Even you wrote bad things about me," she reminded me.

"I was jealous," I admitted. "You and Janelle are so close. And I always felt a little excluded. So I just lashed out. I'm sorry."

Adria and I didn't say anything for a minute or so.

"Have you ever just wanted to disappear?" Adria asked quietly.

I knew this was bad. It wasn't really about what people had written on a website. We all wanted to disappear sometimes. We all occasionally felt sad. But Adria had gone beyond that. She needed help. Help I wasn't qualified to give.

I crept a little closer. I didn't want her to shut down and stop talking. If I could keep her talking, I could figure out what to do.

"Where are your parents?" I asked.

"My dad went to talk to the principal," she said. "My mom went to work."

"The principal?" I asked. "Why?"

"They found out about SlamBook," she said. "They

want the site taken down. I'm sure that's for the best, but it won't fix things. I'll still have to go to school and face people who hate me."

"You see, I don't think that's true," I said. "I saw who was posting bad things. A few people were writing nasty comments for everyone. They just wanted attention. I wrote a few things to get back at them, but nothing they wrote was true. They said Janelle was full of herself. I mean, come on! We both know that is complete crap."

Adria didn't smile. Not even a little. It seemed almost as though she didn't even hear me. I wasn't sure what I could say that would get through, because this was about so much more than SlamBook.

"Have you talked to any grown-ups about how you feel?" I asked. "Your mom? A teacher, maybe?"

"No," she said. "We weren't supposed to tell anyone about SlamBook. My dad knew I was upset, so I said it was about the website, but it's not just that."

I nodded slowly. "Maybe it would help to talk to someone," I said gently. "My mom could help you, if you don't want your parents to get involved. I could even talk to your parents for you."

 216

She nodded, but she still looked dazed. I didn't want to leave her alone, but the good news was, my mom was out there somewhere, maybe even in the hallway. I turned to go get her and saw Hope step into the doorway.

"Do you want me to—?" she whispered.

I nodded. She didn't even have to finish her sentence. We knew each other that well. That was the good thing about having a sister.

Mom came in a few seconds later, passing me to go kneel down beside Adria's bed. "Do you want me to call your mother?" she asked.

"No," Adria said. "I want Faith to do it."

Adria looked up, and we locked eyes. I nodded. Adria pulled up her mom's number and handed me her phone. I went to a different room so they couldn't hear what I said. I wasn't sure what I was doing, but I knew that we'd get Adria the help she needed, and that eased the terror that had been squeezing the breath out of me for days.

CHAPTER 16

"You did the right thing," Hope said one last time as she grabbed the door handle to get out of the car. We'd just pulled up in front of her school—and I still hadn't stopped shaking. I was pretty sure the whole thing with Adria had changed me forever.

We'd stayed with Adria until her mom had gotten there, which wasn't long at all. Turned out, even though her mom had gone to work, she'd been super worried about Adria and had known something wasn't right. She had been so frenzied when she'd gotten there, she hadn't said much at all to us, which made me feel like she was mad at us for getting involved, but Mom had said, no, that wasn't true.

"I don't know what all this SlamBook stuff is about," Mom said. "But what happened with Adria was much more complicated than that. You know that, right?"

"Yes," I said.

But I knew I had to say more. I knew this conversation had to happen *now*.

"I wrote some bad things on SlamBook," I confessed. "I did it out of revenge, but that doesn't make it right. I wrote about people being backstabbers and stuff like that. I even wrote that Adria was a Janelle wannabe."

Mom didn't respond for the longest time. Meanwhile, my heart was pounding so hard, I was half expecting it to jump right out of my chest. I deserved to be in serious trouble for a long, long time. Maybe grounded until I was twenty-one.

"Okay," Mom said. "We're going to have to talk about this later. I'm very proud of you for what you did today, but I'm disappointed in you for giving in to gossip and bullying. You do understand that what you did was bullying, right?"

I understood that SlamBook was bullying, but I'd justified my behavior as bullying the bullies. Which somehow had made it okay to me for a while, but not anymore. Now I realized that all I'd done was just make everything worse.

"Yes," I said quietly, the weight of all I'd done finally catching up to me. I'd spent so much time worrying about Adria, I'd conveniently escaped dealing with the consequences of my actions. I'd escaped dealing with the fact that I was just as much a part of the problem as the people I'd been trying to stop.

"And you're going to do something about it?" Mom asked.

I nodded. I wasn't sure what, and I knew she wouldn't tell me. I had to figure it out for myself, just as I'd done when I'd swiped some candy from the checkout line at the grocery store when I was six. Without my mom having to tell me, I'd walked right up to the cashier and handed it to her. I'd fessed up immediately and apologized.

I had to do that here. I had to figure out a way to make up for making things worse with SlamBook.

CHAPTER 17

The school was empty. Totally empty. It was super weird.

I shouldn't say *totally* empty. My first stop was at the school office, where I signed in and got a slip for being late. I went straight from the office to my first-period classroom, but the hallways were eerily quiet. Not a person in sight.

It was even weirder when I got to first period and the room was empty. No students, no teachers, nothing. I'd been so lost in my thoughts, I hadn't thought to look into the other classrooms as I'd passed. But I stepped into the hall and checked, and sure enough, every classroom was empty.

Weird. It was like I was in one of those sci-fi movies where everyone had vanished at the same time. There had to be a logical explanation, though. Maybe everyone in school had been suspended for SlamBook. Was that possible? Wouldn't the woman in the office have mentioned it when she gave me the late slip? She'd said absolutely nothing, but she had been distracted by ringing phones.

Just as I'd decided to go straight back to the office to ask what was going on, a teacher whose name I didn't know stepped out of one of the rooms. He was staring down at his phone, so he didn't see me.

"Excuse me," I said.

I'd said the words not too loudly, but he jumped a little anyway. He then looked around, as though just then realizing where he was.

"Why aren't you in the assembly?" he asked.

I held up my late slip, then realized what he'd actually said. "Assembly?"

"Everyone's in the auditorium," he said. "You're missing it."

So was *he*, but this wasn't exactly the time to point that out, I decided. I just needed to get to that assembly.

"Thanks," I said, race-walking toward the auditorium.

It was not a short walk. The auditorium was on the total opposite side of the building from my first-period class. And my locker. And the cafeteria. And pretty much anywhere else I went during the day. My race walking soon turned into a run, then an all-out sprint. As I drew closer and started hearing sounds from the auditorium, I slowed to a walk, though. Suddenly I wasn't so eager to slip through those open doors.

There was no question in my mind. This was about SlamBook. I just hoped they hadn't identified who had written what. I crept up to the doorway and stood off to the side, peering in. All I could see were rows of the backs of heads, everyone facing Mr. Marquez, who was standing onstage with a somber look on his face.

"We've tracked down the creator of SlamBook," he said. "And some of you may be surprised. It was created by a student participating in a coding club that some of you here are part of. That student lives on the other side of the country."

Coding club. There was only one club I knew about called that, and that was the one I was involved in. The reality hit me. Hard. I couldn't even move from my spot in the doorway.

Someone in my coding club had done this. A person I'd never met who was doing a project like I was. Since the website had schools from all over the United States on there, things like what had happened to Adria could have been happening to kids all over the country.

I had to talk to Ms. Wang. I couldn't be part of the club if they weren't going to do something about this. I wanted to know that Ms. Wang didn't know that some coding club student had created SlamBook.

But first, I had to face what I'd done.

I scooted into the auditorium, snuck to the last row, and took a seat on the end. Nobody turned to look at me, thank goodness. I wanted to stay invisible for as long as possible.

"But this isn't about what some programming student on the other side of the country did," he said. "This is about you. We're working on getting the information on who set up this school's slam book and who made some of the most inflammatory comments. We're particularly concerned about some racist and body-shaming posts. This isn't what Gladesville Middle is about."

It felt as though the entire school hung its collective head in shame at his comment. I wondered how many people in this auditorium had actually participated. At the very least, most of them probably had read the comments on various pages. I supposed that made them guilty of knowing this was going on and doing nothing to stop it.

"So here's what we're going to do," Mr. Marquez said. "The coding club has made the developer take SlamBook offline while we investigate. Don't bother checking it. You won't find it."

Okay. I imagined the coding club leaders going directly to the person who'd created the site and demanding a list of all accounts. Or maybe they'd have Ms. Wang do it. Whatever the case, everything we'd done would be available for Mr. Marquez and anyone else to see. And there was no way to go in and delete it, because he'd said the site was now offline.

I felt sick. But I also knew it was for the best that Slam-Book was gone. In fact, if they hadn't taken the site offline, I still would have left my comments there. I deserved to pay for them.

"Every person here who posted something negative about someone on SlamBook is going to apologize," Mr.

Marquez said. "To every single person you slammed. Every single person. Do you understand me?"

There were plenty of murmurs and whispering sounds across the auditorium as people tried to work out what that meant. Guaranteed, people were worried that they couldn't remember everyone they'd slammed. Which was pathetic.

"If you miss someone, we'll find out," he said. "We'll discover it when we call that person to the office and show what you wrote. And if you didn't apologize before that time, you'll have me to answer to. *Do you understand?*"

The way he enunciated every word of that last question made it clear that he was mad. Way mad. And all we could do at this point was do what he said. I just wondered what would happen when everyone found out who'd written what about them. I was imagining plenty of people arguing in the school hallways. Lots of fractured friendships, too. This might not be such a good idea.

But I saw the message behind it. There were repercussions for our words, even if we thought those words were anonymous. Even if we thought we were hiding behind a username or number on a website. We had to hold ourselves accountable for that.

I went to Susannah first, only because I found her in the hall right after the assembly. Other people may have been putting off their apologies until later in the day, but I was all about getting it over with.

"I said you smile to people's face while stabbing them in the back," I blurted as I fell into step beside her. "That was me."

There was a reason I'd posted that, but that didn't matter. What did matter was that I'd owned up to what I'd done. It was wrong, no matter what the reason.

Susannah stopped walking and turned to face me. I moved out of the way to avoid being trampled by all the people rushing out of the auditorium to get to class.

"You wrote that?" she said. "That was pretty upsetting."

I wanted to fire back, "So was what you said." But I didn't. This was about me, not her. She'd have to deal with her own wrongs.

"If you wrote something on SlamBook, I'm sure you're in the same position," I did manage to say. "I made mistakes. I'm the first to admit it. And I feel horrible about it."

"Is that how you feel about me?" she asked. "You think I'm not genuine?"

I didn't think she was genuine. Not after I'd seen what she'd written on SlamBook. Before that, I honestly hadn't given her all that much thought.

"I think we're all learning that people aren't who we thought they were," I replied.

She narrowed her eyes at me. "But to write that? I've never talked behind someone's back."

"Are you sure about that?" I asked.

Those narrowed eyes stayed narrowed. Her mouth clamped shut. I could tell she was wondering what I knew. Probably going back through every piece of gossip she'd ever shared. Every nasty thing she'd ever said about a friend. Okay, so I wasn't going to bring up SlamBook, but maybe that was a good thing. Maybe she was thinking about other things she'd done as well.

"You know what, I'm done talking to you," she said. "Don't speak to me again." And then she walked around me and flounced off down the hall like I was the only one who'd done something wrong.

It was so hard, this "being the bigger person" thing. I wanted to point out to her that she'd said bad stuff too, but that was between her and the people she'd wronged. If she refused to own up to it, she'd pay down the line, when everyone found out who had posted what.

Meanwhile, I had to talk to Amy. She would be the hardest one because she legit thought of me as a friend. Or at least a good acquaintance. I saw her at her locker, no sign at all of her usual smile. She looked like she was just seconds away from meeting her doom.

"First of all, let me say I'm so, so, so sorry," I said.

Amy had a confused look on her face as she turned toward me. But then she gave a slow nod, her mouth forming an O. She turned back to her locker and started rearranging her books.

"I got caught up in all the attention that slams were getting people," I said. "I posted some horrible stuff, but I didn't mean a word of it. Well, not completely. I mean, when you're angry, you don't really have a perspective on things, and the day I posted about you, I was angry."

She looked confused again. "Angry about what?" she asked, her attention still on her locker.

"I don't even remember," I said, mostly because I couldn't tell the truth. "I guess it had to do with you being so excited about SlamBook when it was hurting so many people."

"Me?" she shrieked way too loudly. "*I* was excited? You should have seen your face when you were talking about it. It's like the whole thing brought you to life. I was right in what I posted about you."

"What did you write about me?" I asked.

"Check it out yourself," she said. "Number forty-two."

"No, you're number fourteen," I blurted.

Oops. She'd inevitably ask me how I knew her number, and what would I say? I'd have to tell her the truth—that I'd hacked in and figured out who'd posted what. No point in keeping it a secret now.

"I am not," she said. "I'm number forty-two. I wrote that you're a really bad word. I wrote a word that rhymed with the word I meant."

The word she'd written had felt like a punch to my gut. I remembered reading that and wondering why anyone would write that about me. I might have been shy and reserved, but I was never mean to anyone. At least, I didn't think I was.

But wait . . . Amy wasn't number fourteen?

"That's not possible," I said, feeling dazed. "You have to be fourteen."

What was actually happening? I didn't understand at all. I'd been operating all this time under the assumption that I knew everyone's numbers. Had I matched them incorrectly? If so, how much else had I gotten wrong? I had to get with Ms. Wang to figure it out.

"I'd show you, but we can't get back in," she said. "But if I'm lying, you'll know soon enough. So what did you say about me?"

I hung my head a little. Then I just blurted it out.

"Loudmouthed know-it-all try-hard."

She didn't say anything at first. I kept my gaze firmly focused on the floor, afraid to look her in the eye. I was sure that any second now she'd start yelling at me. Or she'd slam her locker door and stomp off in the same direction Susannah had gone. Instead she laughed.

Yes, laughed. I couldn't believe it at first. I looked up and verified that she was, indeed, laughing. Not at all what I'd expected.

Shaking her head while her laughter subsided a little, she closed her locker door and turned to face me. "That's awesome," she said.

"I'm sorry," I said. "So, so sorry. It was wrong."

Her smile faltered a little, and she just stared at me for what seemed like the longest time. "I'm sorry too," she finally said. "I got caught up in all of it and . . . well, I was just wrong."

I smiled as we went our separate ways. Maybe Susannah would stay mad at me, but at least Amy and I were on somewhat good terms.

Before I could feel better, though, I looked around. As I walked to my second-period class, I passed fight after fight after fight. But then I saw hugs, too. The apologies seemed like they weren't going well for everyone, but at least some people were okay.

I wondered if maybe Mr. Marquez had been wrong about us getting all this out into the open. Sure, it had been bad that we'd said those things about each other, but was admitting it all to each other's faces just going to cause even more trouble? It seemed like it was . . . for some people, anyway.

Suddenly I remembered Janelle. I'd been so caught up in everything, I'd totes forgotten about her. I pulled my phone from my pocket as I rushed to class, and sure enough, there was a series of texts from her. I spotted Adria's name as I skimmed them—Janelle just wanted an update—and I typed a reply as I walked.

Me: **Her mom's with her. She'll get the help she needs.**

Then I pocketed the phone and rushed off to class. I didn't check it again until the bell rang and I was on my way to lunch. That was when I saw Janelle's panicked responses.

Janelle: **What do U mean by help? Whaaaaaaat?**

This was something I had to talk to her about. In person. I couldn't describe in a text message what had happened that morning.

Fortunately, she was waiting for me right outside the door to the cafeteria. She looked so anxious, I felt horrible for not finding her earlier. I'd been so busy trying to make the whole SlamBook thing right, I'd forgotten that Janelle was worried about her BFF.

"She's fine," I said. "She's going to be fine. She's with her mom."

"You said," she said in a not-so-nice voice. "What the heck is going on?"

"She's really depressed," I said. "It's about more than

SlamBook. I mean, I'm sure SlamBook didn't help things, but this is more a clinical thing."

"I'm going over there," she said. "I need to talk to her."

"I don't even know if she's home," I said.

What if her mom had taken her to the doctor or something? That was so private. I didn't really want to get into the ins and outs of depression with Janelle.

"Google 'depression,'" I said, pointing at her phone. "She's sick. It's like she has an illness and they need to treat it. Understand?"

I could tell from the look on her face that she didn't understand at all. Nor did she want to. She wasn't getting it.

"She'll be fine," she said. "I'll talk to her. Once she hears SlamBook is gone, she'll snap out of it."

I shook my head. "No, she won't. You don't 'snap out of' depression. Seriously. And talk to your mom about it. This is serious. She needs help."

I breathed a sigh of relief when Janelle finally seemed to get it. Her jaw loosened its clench a little and her eyes softened. She looked off the side, like she was processing what I'd just said.

"What can I do?" she asked quietly.

She was looking at me now. When did I become the expert on this stuff? I wasn't. But I'd read up on it, and I thought I maybe knew the answer. Either way, hopefully Adria's mom would get the information she needed and be able to help.

"Just be there for her," I said. "Let her know you're there. That's all you really can do right now."

She nodded. "I'm going to go call my mom and see if I can leave," she said.

She started to walk off. I'd go see Adria after school. I'd let her know I was there for her too, although I was pretty sure she already knew. Right then Adria needed her mom and best friend, and it was important not to get in the way of that.

Suddenly Janelle stopped, midstep, and turned to look at me.

"Thanks," she said. "Thanks for everything you did."

As she walked off, there were tears in my eyes. I had no idea if I'd "done" anything. I'd pretty much just handed Adria over to her mother. I'd done my own awful things on SlamBook. I couldn't feel good about anything I'd done for Adria. All I knew was that I felt a little better that

Adria was in the right hands now. I couldn't have gone about my day otherwise.

I headed into the cafeteria, my heart heavy, not even really caring about the tense atmosphere in there. There were much more important things than the fact that everyone in our school was suddenly fighting. I just went to the line, ordered my food, paid, and headed for the table where Janelle, Adria, and I normally sat.

Nobody was there. It wasn't just Janelle's and Adria's seats—I'd expected those to be empty. But the tables on either side were empty. In fact, all around, there were empty seats everywhere. It was so weird.

There were people eating, sure. But things were all rearranged. People were sitting alone all over the place. But there were plenty of people laughing and chatting like everything was fine. I wondered if those were the people who had apologized and moved on. Or were they the ones who hadn't even been involved with SlamBook?

"Is this seat taken?"

Just when I'd resigned myself to eating my lunch solo, Tierra appeared, tray in hand, looking almost shy. "Not at all," I said. "Thank you."

I didn't really understand why I was thanking her. The words just slipped out. I supposed I was thanking her for continuing to speak to me despite the fact that I'd screwed up our friendship so much.

"How's Adria?" she asked before she'd even taken her seat. She settled her tray in front of her, centering it carefully before picking up her fork.

"It's as we thought," I said, then corrected myself. "*Feared*. Her mom is with her now. I'm hoping she'll get Adria the help she needs."

"Yeah," Tierra said, shoveling a forkful of peas into her mouth before chewing thoughtfully for a moment. "So . . ."

"Thank you for your help," I said. "I just . . . I can't do any of this without you."

She stared at me for a long moment. It wasn't an apology, though. I owed her an apology, didn't I?

"You know, I get that friends drift apart," she said. "But you could have talked to me about it. To just stop speaking to me? I thought we were closer than that."

"We were," I said. "I just . . ."

"You had the chance to sit at the popular table," Tierra

said. "I get it. But, you know, there's more to life than being popular."

I nodded. I got that now. I'd learned so much from SlamBook. Mostly it was that no matter who we were, we all had our insecurities. Even Janelle.

"I've missed you," I said. "Nobody gets me like you do."

She smiled. "I've missed you, too. And I'm hoping maybe you can teach me some of that coding stuff. I'd love to learn."

I smiled back. With everything happening, it was nice to just smile for a second. I couldn't help but think too how good nice words could actually make me feel. It was like the opposite of SlamBook.

"The opposite of SlamBook!" I said out loud. *Very* out loud. As in, "people all around us turned to look at us" loud.

"What?" Tierra asked between chews.

"I think I know what we need to do," I said. "But I need your help."

CHAPTER 18

"Are we ready?" I asked.

I looked to my right and saw Janelle. To my left was Tierra. They both were staring at the front of the school, directly in front of us. We linked hands and walked toward the entrance.

The door swung open just as we reached it. Adria looked out at us, a shaky smile on her face. She'd gotten the key from a friend who worked in the office. We all felt a little shaky that early Saturday morning. This was a big, big moment.

But together, we could do this.

Just inside the door, past Adria, was one of those carts that teachers were always pushing around the hallways. Stacked as high as they could go were pads of sticky notes, each unwrapped and ready for writing.

"We'll leave it here," I said, pushing the cart up against the wall. I couldn't 100 percent guarantee this cart would remain here on Monday morning, but I was pretty confident that once Mr. Marquez saw what we'd done, he'd want to support us.

"Let's get started," Adria said, handing out Sharpies. We each grabbed a sticky pad and started writing.

"Wait," Tierra said. "What do we write?"

"Uplifting messages," I said. "Imagine a time when you just needed some encouraging words."

"You matter," Adria said. She held up the note she'd just written, then stuck it on the wall, pressing down to make sure it stayed.

"Believe in yourself," Janelle said.

"You can do it?" Tierra asked. "Is that too close to what you guys are saying?"

"These are going to cover this entire wall," I said, pointing to the humungous blank canvas in front of us.

"It can be similar. Just put it a little farther away."

We all started furiously writing and sticking. Messages like *You are loved* and *Mistakes make you wiser*. At some point, Janelle even pulled out her phone and gave us a few.

"Need help?"

We were so caught up in what we were doing, we didn't even know that someone else was in the hall with us until we heard a voice behind us. I turned and saw Amy standing there. Behind her was a large group of students, including Susannah and Damen King.

"We got your invitation," Amy said. "We're here to help."

The four of us looked at each other. None of us had sent an invitation.

"Ms. Wang did a whole thing," Amy said. "It's in place of SlamBook."

While my friends passed out sticky pads and Sharpies, I pulled out my phone and looked up SlamBook. Sure enough, there was a page there in place of the *Our website is offline* notice that had been there just a couple of days before. The page had the title "The Kindness Project" in big, bold letters at the top.

Below it was an invitation for every SlamBook school to show up and do exactly what we were doing. Sticky note walls, with uplifting quotes to help every student who passed by feel just a little better. As the page Ms. Wang had created said, we were making the world a better place, one sticky note at a time.

I knew where all this had come from too. After the assembly, I'd called Ms. Wang and we'd had a long talk about SlamBook. She'd known nothing about the project one of the coding club members was creating. Even that kid's own mentor hadn't realized it. He'd been kicked out as soon as they'd found out, but the damage had already been done.

I'd also had her look into the number mishap. Turned out, number fourteen had used Amy's name as a fake name when signing up. We didn't know who that person was, but the other names had been right. The real Amy had used a nickname, and I didn't recognize it, so I'd just glossed right over it when I was matching up numbers.

When I'd come up with the idea for the Kindness Project, I'd called Ms. Wang up to ask what she thought about it. So it was no surprise that she'd helped out. She just hadn't given me the specifics.

"Hey," Adria said to me. "Can we talk for a second?"

I was a little surprised. Adria had hung out with us a little since I'd gone to her house, but she'd opened up mostly to Janelle. Janelle was the one keeping us updated on how Adria was doing now, which was better every day, thanks to the help she was getting. I figured she probably wanted to talk to me about the project, but something about her demeanor made me think it was much more than that.

We slipped into an empty classroom nearby, and Tierra closed the door behind us. That confirmed it. This wasn't about the project.

"I just wanted to thank you for helping me," Adria said. "I never got the chance to say that. I'm so grateful."

I reached out and touched her arm. "We're friends too," I said. "I know we kind of connected through Janelle, but I want us to get to know each other better outside of our friendship with Janelle. Can we do that?"

She smiled. This time the smile reached all the way to her eyes. I hadn't seen it do that in a long, long time.

"I'd like that," she said. "I'd like that very much."

By the time we got back to the hallway, the wall was

filling up with sticky notes. There was a rainbow of colors, each note with its own different message written in black Sharpie.

"We have to leave space," I called out, suddenly worried that there would be nowhere for other students to add their own sayings when they saw this on Monday.

Janelle stepped back and admired the work in progress. "I think that's enough," she said.

"One more," Adria said, stepping forward to grab a sticky note and pen from the cart.

While Janelle and I watched, Adria wrote just a few words on the note.

You can do anything with friends by your side, she wrote.

"Perfect!" I said.

Gradually people wandered out, leaving just the four of us standing in front of our wall. I wondered what Mr. Marquez would say when he saw it. He wouldn't have to wait until Monday. Janelle snapped a few photos and shared them online, so chances were, he'd know all about it by the time the weekend was over. I had a feeling he'd be very proud.

"Anyone up for a movie?" Janelle asked, looking around at the three of us.

"I have to volunteer at the church," Tierra said. "But you guys go have fun. I'll catch you later?"

"Actually," I said, suddenly feeling an urge I hadn't expected. "I'd like to go to the church too. Senior poker sounds like just what I need right now."

Adria looked at Janelle and said, "You know, that senior poker thing does sound kind of fun. You in?"

"You do know we just help the seniors," Tierra said. "We don't get to play."

"Yeah, it's just . . ." Adria hesitated. "I feel like everyone's been so good to me. I want to pay it back, you know?"

Yes, I knew exactly. We all had spent a lot of time lately trying to pay things back.

"I'm in!" Janelle said. "Let's go."

We locked arms and walked toward Janelle's mom's car, which was parked in front of the school. I couldn't wait to see how the new SlamBook would turn our school around.

ACKNOWLEDGMENTS

When I was in junior high, someone handed me a notebook that had a page with my name at the top. It was called a slam book, I was told, and people could write things about you. There was a list of nice comments about me, with only one negative one, but I still remember that negative comment today.

I owe a debt of thanks to whatever student created that book, probably inspired by an episode of *Facts of Life* that included it as a subplot. That book taught me important lessons about how we tend to hear the negative things people say about us more than the positive. Although writing is a tough journey, the friends we make along the way make it easier. Those friends are the ones who support us during the highs and lows.

My writing friends keep me going, helping me get unstuck when the words just won't come and providing general support and advice along the way. Gail, Debbie, Grace, Melissa, Porscha, and Alicia—I couldn't do it without you.

I also owe a huge thanks to my amazing editor, Alyson, and the entire Aladdin team. Each book is made a thousand times stronger thanks to their support. My agent, Natalie, is always there to give feedback on ideas and cheer me on when I'm on the right path.

Then there's family. I'm so lucky to have my husband, Neil, who supports me in everything I do. My mother, Valerie, and sister, Jennifer, are always there for me, and their love means everything. You can do anything with friends and family by your side.

ABOUT THE AUTHOR

Stephanie Faris is the author of the middle-grade books *30 Days of No Gossip* and *25 Roses* as well as the Piper Morgan chapter book series. When she isn't writing books for children, she writes technology, finance, and business content for a variety of websites. She currently lives in her hometown, just north of Nashville. Visit her online at StephanieFaris.com.